ABOUT THIS BOOK

The anticipated sequel to *Nowhere to Hide* continues the story of Sedona and Micah.

As Havenwood Falls' resident bookstore owner, empath Sedona Mathews is surrounded by a swirling mess of feelings—both fictional and real. But until now, they'd always belonged to others. Then sexy angel Micah Westbrook walked into her bookstore and her life. After a surprising twist of events, she finds herself head over heels in love with him, and no longer vicariously living through the romance novels she reads and sells. Sedona's deeply embroiled in her very own story, with strong, intense, passionate desires erupting from inside her and throwing her world into chaos and mischief.

Love.

Infatuation.

Lust.

Addiction.

The trouble with emotions, however, is that in the space of a minute, they can twist and change—complicating life in a heartbeat. When Sedona's hunger for Micah pushes her over the edge, she soon realizes just how much she's neglected her abilities. But after the recent betrayal and attack in Shelf Indulgence and rumors circulating about the mysterious Collector, Sedona must figure out if her new attitude toward Micah is really part of the journey, or if there's something more sinister at work.

HAVENWOOD FALLS BOOKS

Forget You Not by Kristie Cook

Old Wounds by Susan Burdorf

Fate, Love & Loyalty by E.J. Fechenda

The Winged & the Wicked by T.V. Hahn & Kristie Cook

Alpha's Queen by Lila Felix

Ink & Fire by R.K. Ryals

Lose You Not by Kristie Cook

Tragic Ink by Heather Hildenbrand

Nowhere to Hide by Belinda Boring

Flames Among the Frost by Amy Hale

Rock Me Gently by Susan Burdorf

From the Embers by Amy Miles

Defying Gravity by Kallie Ross

Break Me Not by Kristie Cook

How the Dead Lie by Stacey Rourke

The Lurkers Within by Danielle Bannister

The Collector: Awakening by Kristie Cook, R.K. Ryals, Belinda Boring & Nadirah Foxx

Addicted to You by Belinda Boring

Affliction Mine by C.J. Pinard

The Ward & the Wanderers by T.V. Hahn

Toil & Trouble by Melissa Wright

Of Salt and Stars by Seven Jane

Redefined by Morgan Wylie

Betrayal Among the Frost by Amy Hale

Forever Loyal by E.J. Fechenda

Fate's Demand by Emily Cyr

The Wu & the Wand by T.V. Hahn

A Demon's Redemption by JD Nelson

Also try the YA line, Havenwood Falls High; the historical paranormal line, Legends of Havenwood Falls; the darker, sexier side of town, Havenwood Falls Sin & Silk; and the local supernatural college, Sun & Moon Academy.

Stay up to date at www.HavenwoodFalls.com

ALSO BY BELINDA BORING

THE MYSTIC WOLVES SERIES

The Mystic Wolves

Forget Me Not

Testing Fate

Forever Changed

Savage Possession

Darkness Unleashed

Last Wolf Standing

Blood Oath

A Very Mystic Christmas (Collection of Christmas Memories)

DAMAGED SOULS SERIES

Bittersweet Melody

Bittersweet Symphony

Enchanted Heart

Loving Liberty

Broken Promises

HAVENWOOD FALLS TITLES

Nowhere to Hide

Addicted to You (Sequel to Nowhere to Hide)

Blood & Damnation (Legends of Havenwood Falls)

The Collector: Awakening

Short Story Anthology 2018

ADDICTED TO YOU

A HAVENWOOD FALLS NOVELLA

BELINDA BORING

To my dear friend and fellow author, Kristie Cook.
Thank you for inviting me to join this incredible world.
You helped me find my joy and voice again. Love you!

CHAPTER 1

"The sooner you hire someone, the sooner things can go back to normal," Maxwell's gruff admonition broke the silence. My ghostly friend had been studying me all morning, and now he was peering around me to the ignored paperwork by the bookstore's computer.

It had been a long, grief-stricken four weeks since the psychic fair and the attack afterwards. Just one short month since I'd been shot and betrayed by someone I'd trusted so completely that I hadn't seen it coming.

I still hadn't brought myself to enter the storage area.

I still hadn't found the courage to sort through the pile of applications stacked on the counter beside me. I wasn't going to rush it. I prayed that my faith could be bigger than my fear, and so far, it was working. One step at a time.

Micah was the one who put away orders as they came in, and he was the one who worked on the to-do list I created each morning. I saw the worry in his eyes whenever I handed it to him, the way his lips kind of parted as though he was about to speak but thought better of it. He understood that I was processing things in my own way, in my own time. The consideration made me love him just that little bit more.

Love could be deadly for an empath.

I knew that painfully well, having lost both my parents to heartbreak. It was a mantra that I'd repeated over and over inside my head, but since meeting Micah Westbrook, there was an even louder voice in my head trying to convince me that it would be one hell of a way to go.

Micah.

The man made it worth the risk.

Maxwell, on the other hand, was not as kind or sympathetic.

I let out a weary sigh and covered the job applications with a magazine.

"Out of sight, out of mind," I countered, not ready to deal with him either today. There was no question that my friendly ghost was struggling as well in the aftermath. His sense of helplessness had been etched across his furrowed brow as he recounted how much he hated not being corporeal. I'd listened to his furious diatribe about Austin, and the only way his temper had been somewhat placated was knowing that Austin had been banished from Havenwood Falls. He'd simply wished for a chance to exact his own justice—the wringing of the traitor's neck.

His words. Not mine.

He'd felt the betrayal keenly because he had stepped in to fill my late grandfather's shoes and watch over me. After I'd discovered the Dunlap Broadside in one of his trunks up in the attic, the truth had come out that not only had my friend been there at the first printing of the Declaration of Independence, but he'd then gone on to fight alongside General George Washington in Yorktown. There was no doubt in my mind that he'd seen all manner of brutality fighting against the English, and had he been able to, he'd have killed Austin with his bare hands.

It had revealed a savagery in him that I'd never witnessed before. I felt like I was meant to be scared of him because of it. Instead, I felt safer. Ghost or not, Maxwell was not a man to be meddled with.

"So you're back to sticking your head in the sand. I see." He didn't bother camouflaging the disappointment in his voice.

My hand hit the top of the counter a little harder than I intended.

"What do you expect me to do?" I asked, my voice filled with exasperation. "I'm not a robot. I can't just experience something . . ." A large lump formed in my throat, making it difficult to swallow and speak. I cleared my throat and tried again. "I can't just bounce back like nothing happened, Maxwell. Why can't you just let me do things in my own time?"

Compassion flooded his gaze, and I could see he desperately wished he could wrap his arms around me in a hug. "Girl, I wish I could. I wish I could say we lived in a world where nothing bad happens and good people live happily ever after. Would you rather I lie to you?"

He peered deeply into my eyes until I could feel him touch my soul. His honesty helped soothe some of the jagged pieces still too raw to mend.

I glanced at the applications again. Here was my opportunity to be equally as candid—to share what was truly at the root of my hesitation.

"What if I make another mistake? What if I don't see the danger and next time it's more . . ." I struggled to finish my sentence.

"Fatal?" The man had read my mind perfectly.

I nodded. "I'm not being morbid or anything, but if it were just me at risk, it wouldn't be too big of an issue. But Holly was there. Micah and I are together now, so she's always going to be around. Micah had tried warning me about the threats he was protecting her from, and I contributed to it." The words came tumbling out with such a force, I was breathless at the end.

Micah's voice surprised me. "Is that what you think?"

Somewhere in the back of my mind, I'd heard the tinkling of the doorbell, but I'd been so wrapped up in my thoughts and conversation with Maxwell that I'd missed Micah entering. The very sight of him made my heart race a bazillion miles an hour, and without thinking, I licked my lips in anticipation.

Kissing was the last thing on his mind, however.

Right now, he pretty much mirrored the exact same expression the ghost did—incredulous shock.

I guess I hadn't confessed that small tidbit to them—my feeling that the attack was my fault and that somehow I should've been able to prevent it.

I shrugged my shoulders, not ready to face both of them about this. "Austin was my employee, my responsibility. It was my store. *I* provided the chance for him and Holly to meet. *I* encouraged their friendship and study dates. How much clearer does it need to be?" I'd gone over the details countless times in my head, often while I lay awake at night, staring up at the ceiling in my apartment. "You know I'm right."

Micah actually scoffed, making a sound that was a cross between a snort and a grunt. "I know you are wrong. One hundred percent, emphatically wrong." He took a step closer, so he could cradle my cheek with his palm. "Sedona, please tell me you don't honestly believe that."

As much as I savored the warmth of his touch, I knew in this moment, with these guilt-riddled feelings churning inside me, it didn't feel right to accept such kindness. Reluctantly, I stepped back and broke the contact.

Micah stared down at where I'd just been standing, a serious look of sadness crossing his handsome features. I hated the fact that I'd been the one to put that expression there. I just didn't know how else to explain what had been bottled up inside me until now.

Maxwell disappeared once he realized this was a private moment. His only parting gift was to mouth the words *listen to him.*

Micah reached for me again, and I skirted away.

"Please don't do that, Sedona. Don't close yourself off from me."

I couldn't help it. I burst into a laugh that bordered on hysterical. "This coming from the man who walked through those doors practically a blank slate, a man with so many secrets that I'm surprised you're not drowning in them all." I could feel my skin heat from the emotional outburst, but I didn't suppress it. "Even now, after everything we've been through, you still keep parts of yourself shielded from me."

There was a hint of frustration in his response. I could feel him trying to be patient and understanding, but like every other man on the planet, he couldn't see it from my perspective.

"This isn't about me, though. We're talking about you." And with all the skill of a ballroom dancer, he sidestepped around my retort, and waltzed me back to where the spotlight was back on me. "Help me comprehend what's going on in that beautiful head of yours." He offered me a gentle smile to try to soften the mood, but it was too late. Everything I'd kept stuffed inside was rushing to the surface, ready to explode.

"Don't flatter me!" I exclaimed. Part of me knew it was unfair to unleash on the man I was dating, the man I was falling in love with. Another part egged my own impatience on, telling me to purge until there was nothing left but the echoes of an empty heart. Surprisingly, there was another voice that had recently emerged. It was that voice that whispered if there was ever a person I could completely confide in and bare my soul to, it would be Micah.

"I'm sorry," he murmured and reached for me again. This time I didn't shrink away.

"Don't you think it's ironic that you expect such transparency from me, yet you keep everything within you tightly wrapped up in some impenetrable fortress?" When he nodded, not speaking a word in response, I took courage. "I may be an empath, but I'm also human, Micah. How else am I meant to feel? Tell me, how am I meant to process this? What must I do so we can all go back to pretending like the world is wonderful and filled with rainbows and butterflies?" I stared up into his deep blue eyes, the challenge thrown. When he didn't reply, I let out a loud, unladylike grunt. "That's what I thought."

Scooping up the damn applications, I gripped them in one hand as I grabbed my keys and threw them at him. "Lock up after yourself. I can't stand being here a second longer."

With one last look over my shoulder, I fled Shelf Indulgence, not waiting to see if he'd follow.

So much for me being okay with what happened and being strong.

Being an empath wasn't as fun as it sounded. It was taxing—both emotionally and physically—and often when I slipped up and invaded someone's feelings (by accident), the consequences resulted in me feeling like an outcast.

Micah had offered to help heal those emotional wounds with his own angelic grace, but I'd politely declined. Every time he used his powers—for whatever reason—it sent out a beacon to those who were hunting for him and Holly. I was grateful that he'd given me a small vial of his divine essence that I wore around my neck, under my clothing. It replaced the black tourmaline pendant I used to wear, but had given to Holly to help ground her after Austin's attack.

Micah's gift was precious to me, and I didn't need to think too hard to know that given time, scars would fade, and it would almost be like my young employee's betrayal had never happened.

Almost.

I could deal with almost.

I'd spent so much time hiding away in my bookstore, sheltering the town from my troublesome gifts, that I'd forgotten just how powerful I could be. Looking down the barrel of the gun Austin had pointed at me, threatening to take Holly away, I'd made a silent vow that should we survive, I would never make myself that vulnerable again.

But that was then and this was now.

It seemed like I was surrounded by lies at the moment, but none bigger than the ones I was telling myself.

I wasn't doing fine.

I was falling apart, and for the life of me, I couldn't stop the tears that finally started to fall.

CHAPTER 2

I didn't get too far before I heard someone calling out after me. It wasn't Micah, because I was pretty sure he was still rooted to the spot in the store, stunned over the tantrum I'd just thrown, his gaze flickering between the door I'd stormed out of and the keys I'd thrown at him.

Embarrassment warred with the guilt that had taken up residence inside me. It took every ounce of willpower for me not to turn around and begin apologizing profusely. I'd acted like a jerk and taken my insecurities out on him.

But I didn't stop. Tears streamed down my cheeks, big salty drops hanging from my top lip before falling. They tasted like regret and fury. Now that I'd lifted the lid on the box that was my own feelings, there was no stuffing them back in.

"Sedona. Please. Don't make me chase after you in these shoes. I won't ever forgive you!"

Callie.

I'd run past the consignment store, and of course, she'd seen me racing by, a complete mess. She wasn't someone who gossiped, and I didn't need my empathic gifts to recognize her intentions. She was worried, and her chasing after me came from a place of compassion.

Slowing down, I shortened my stride and gave her a chance to catch up. A few moments later, her arm looped through mine, and her friendly energy reached out calmly. It was enough to bring me to a complete halt.

I didn't deserve this kindness.

Not now.

Not today.

A lie started forming in my mind. The last thing I wanted was to have a complete meltdown in the town square instead of going somewhere more private, like I'd hoped.

But there was no holding back my emotions now as I sniffled, tempted to wipe my nose on the back of my hand, grossness be damned. Luckily, Callie had come prepared with not just one tissue, but the entire box.

"Here. Knock yourself out." She didn't study me too hard, and I was grateful for that. We stood there together—side by side—before I started walking again. This time it lacked the frenetic pace from before. The anger and bluster had ebbed, and like the tide, it swept back out from my heart.

"Sorry," I murmured, picking a spot on the ground to focus on. That was the thing about holding someone's gaze. If you knew what you were looking for, you could read a person's mind and get a sense of what they were feeling. You didn't need to be magical or an empath. You just needed to be patient enough for the truth to reveal itself.

Callie understood.

I wasn't ready to be that vulnerable with her.

Taking a deep breath, I blew my nose again, and attempted to steady the riot that had exploded inside me. I felt chaotic. All it had taken was a small tap-tap at the wall, and a crack had appeared in the dam around my psyche.

I hated feeling like this—so out of control and uncertain.

"You're going to think I'm being stupid," I began, hoping she'd believe the fib I was about to give her. "It's this freaking purple pig plate design I've been working on." Casting a quick sideways glance at my friend, I silently hoped she wouldn't ask too many questions.

"You mean for Plate Painting in the Park?" Callie asked, her surprise showing. "That's the reason you're rushing down the street like someone kicked your dog?" The strength in her stare almost unraveled my nerve. "Sedona, it's all about having fun. I'm sure your plate's going to kick ass like usual."

For a second there, I thought she was talking to someone else, because while I had many talents, artistic skill with a paintbrush was not one of them. I'd be lucky if the traditional pig even resembled one.

"I'm surprised the witch hasn't come back to haunt me." A few more fat tears rolled over my cheeks, and I snorted. "Her plates sucked souls into the painted scenes. Mine just suck."

There were many traditions here in Havenwood Falls, and despite my exaggeration, I actually enjoyed the plate painting event held in April. I'd been doodling for the past few months, hoping that inspiration would strike, and maybe, just maybe, this was the year *my* design would be featured. It hadn't happened yet, but a girl could dream.

Callie stood there silently, studying me.

She cut straight to the chase. "Liar."

"Excuse me?" I fired back. The sinking sensation in my gut told me she'd seen right through my story. I couldn't lie to save my life.

"You heard me. I don't believe that's why you're *this* upset." Callie refused to break eye contact with me, and my resolve weakened.

"I'm an empath," I blurted. "I feel things passionately and deeply." My cheeks were starting to tingle from the cool air hitting them. Whereas most of the country was beginning to warm up, with spring melting away the last effects of winter, the weather in Havenwood Falls was still quite brisk. The forecast app I had on my phone had warned me not to expect anything higher than forty degrees today, so I'd dressed warmly. Right now, I wanted to wrap my black crocheted scarf around my face.

"I think we need to go on an excursion." Callie spoke so matter-of-factly that I didn't argue. Instead, I let her guide me around the town's square until we stopped in front of Eloise's shop, Into The Mystic. It housed all kinds of new-age things, including psychic readings.

My tears had finally abated, and I rubbed at my tired eyes, wishing we were standing in front of my apartment door instead. The sudden need for the privacy of my own home was overwhelming, but when I went to step back, Callie clicked her tongue in disapproval.

"Be brave, dear friend." And with that, she pushed me through the door, the smell of white sage incense hitting me square in the face.

"But," I began, trying to explain that this was the last place I wanted to be. Memories of the fair and the events that happened afterward tugged sharply at my heart, and more tears filled my eyes. Eloise had organized the fair, and while it wasn't her fault, everything associated with that night and my being shot made it tainted for me.

Callie stopped guiding me, and instead turned me about so she could face me. Her eyes were more hazel today than the green they usually were. There was such a confidence bursting from within them that I wished I could somehow reach down inside her and claim some for myself.

"Do you trust me?"

I was slow to answer, purposely trying to avoid eye contact. "You don't . . ."

She cut me off, not wanting to hear the excuse I was prepared to deliver. "Yes or no, Sedona. Do you trust me?"

This time I threw aside the fear that had controlled me and boldly kept her gaze. "Yes."

"Then believe me when I say you need this." She wore that same expression again—the one that said she was one hundred percent certain that what she spoke was truth. She'd read my cards at the fair, and while a lot was just teasing, there had been tidbits that struck close to home.

Like my growing love for Micah and my worry about getting my heart broken. Tarot had counseled me to take a risk and dare to fly— that the only thing holding me back from finding the happiness I craved was myself.

I let out a pent-up breath and nodded. "Fine."

I looked about the store, noting the new Van Morrison poster Eloise had hung up by the cash register. Every book Shelf Indulgence had ever sold about the Irish singer and songwriter had been ordered just for her. In fact, I recognized the lyrics to his song, Into the Mystic, which was oddly fitting, considering the store's name.

"What am I looking for?" I asked, trying not to sound like a petulant child. What I also didn't admit was that I was already feeling better. It meant there would be no wallowing at home with a large glass of wine and a book, hiding under a blanket fort in the living room. My emotions were no longer clouding my judgment.

I was back to feeling more like me.

"You need another talisman," Callie replied promptly, and with a sweeping gesture of her hand, she pointed over to one of my favorite parts of the store. "Go find the one that calls out to you."

Crystals.

Gems.

Stones.

It didn't matter what you called them, it was the energy and magic that was contained within them, a small piece of Mother Earth to hold and keep close.

"We could be here a while," I whispered softly, wonder now filling my voice as I slowly began tuning everything else out. I felt lured to the neat shelves and baskets that contained the different stones. There was an ever-so-slight tug at my aura—that telltale sign that what I was looking for was also seeking me.

I lightly touched a beautiful green stone and read the card in front of it. Malachite, a stone that had incredible healing properties to the one wearing it. Electricity zapped at my fingertips, revealing its power, but it wasn't the one calling me.

Callie nodded as I moved away from her, the movement caught in my peripheral vision. "I'll be here whenever you're ready."

And with that, she turned her focus to the tarot and oracle cards that were arranged on a nearby shelf.

We were both content to explore.

Quartz.

Citrine.

Snowflake Obsidian.

Selenite.

Each of these crystals caught my eye and warmed my hand as I held them. Snippets of information filled my mind—lessons where I'd learned how one helped reduce stress while another was good for canceling out negative energy. I remembered my grandfather telling me that selenite was a great stone to include in my collection because it didn't require charging from the full moon, adding his warning that should I submerge one in water, it might dissolve.

Selenite had always intrigued me. The one before me had been cut and polished to resemble a unicorn horn, and I could already feel its cleansing energy brushing across my aura. It held the ability of promoting clarity to a troubled mind, yet when I picked it up, closing my eyes to see if it was the *one*, I felt sadly empty.

It was only after walking down a few feet and looking to the left that I found it—the stone that beckoned like a siren, its frequency pinging hard against my own.

I didn't need to read the neatly written card to know its name.

Labradorite, or what I affectionately called it, the galaxy stone.

To some, under a certain light, it appeared to be a dull piece of rock, somewhat transparent with a greenish, black color. But when you held it a certain way, the most gorgeous flashes of color burst outward. Greens, blues, yellows, and sometimes, if you were lucky, you could find purples and pinks.

I tentatively reached out to the palm-sized stone, marveling at how it fit so perfectly. As I curled my fingers around it, appreciating the bold flashes of blues and greens, I felt the most incredible heat flow through my veins, sweeping throughout my body until it burst out the top of my head.

I felt energized.

I felt grounded.

I felt it caress the wounds I'd received to my spirit and gently heal them.

I'd found my new talisman.

"Excellent choice," Eloise interjected from behind me. It didn't bother me that she surprised me. Nothing else mattered but the soothing feeling that all but encompassed me, acting like a salve on my bruised heart.

Callie had made her way back over to me as well. "Labradorite. I should've known. It's all about persevering through the changes and learning to trust your intuition again, Sedona."

Eloise nodded, her graying auburn hair pulled back into a soft bun. The Swarovski crystals in her dangly earrings caught the light from above and glittered. "You'll find the answers you seek. Don't give up."

Satisfied with her contribution to the conversation, she excused herself to help the other customer who was perusing. That was Eloise Sinclair for you. She was eccentric, and psychic, and you might not always understand her meaning, but when she said something with that prophetic tone, you listened.

"Feeling better?" Callie asked, nudging me with her shoulder. "Is it working its magic?" Her eyes dropped to the crystal I now held up to my chest.

I laughed. An hour ago, I would've thought such a response impossible. I'd been consumed by pain and fear. While it wasn't all rainbows and sunshine yet, I was definitely seeing clearer.

"Thank you."

Callie shrugged it off. "What are friends for?" It was then that she revealed what she was holding. A bundle of white sage leaves wrapped with twine. "I officially declare this excursion a success." She returned to guiding me, knowing that I wouldn't be handing over the crystal, my fingers still wrapped around its smooth surface. "Eloise, could you put this all on my tab?" Callie raised the sage and pointed to me.

"No," I started, shaking my head. "You don't need to do that, Callie. I can pay for it." I was already reaching for the debit card stashed in the front pocket of my jeans.

She actually looked like she was ready to scold me. "Consider it a congratulations gift." She dared to wiggle her eyebrows at me, her eyes twinkling. "And no, I'm not going to tell you what I mean. You'll know soon enough."

Damn psychics with their cryptic comments.

There was no arguing with her. "Then, thank you again." I offered her a watery smile, my eyes filling this time with grateful tears. I started laughing again and quickly wiped them away. "I'm such a mess."

"But you're a cute one," she countered. Handing me the small brown paper bag that held the smudging bundle, she waved goodbye to Eloise. I followed quickly after.

We slowly walked back toward her consignment store and my bookstore in comfortable silence, and I relished the peace that had settled within me.

True peace.

Welcomed peace.

"Do you need me to come in with you?" Callie asked as we reached Shelf Indulgence. The lights were out, which told me that Micah had closed everything up like I'd requested—demanded. Guilt tugged again at me for my rudeness toward him, and I was glad that he wasn't still there waiting for me to return. I needed a little more time to pull myself together, and I wanted to do this next part alone.

It was long overdue.

I shook my head slowly.

"I've got this," I said, my voice growing stronger and more self-assured. Suddenly I turned and threw my arms around her. "You knew exactly what I needed, Callie. Thank you so much." I squeezed her one more time before releasing her. "I . . ." I was at a loss for words again. "Did you know the Beatles released their song 'A Little Help From My Friends' on the tenth anniversary of International Friendship Day?"

A knowing smile curled her lips. "And you'll always have mine, Sedona."

Before it became too awkward with me standing there reciting more facts instead of expressing how I felt, I patted the side of my jeans, groaning out loud.

"Micah has the keys, doesn't he?" She said it more as a fact than a question.

I closed my eyes momentarily before remembering I'd stashed a separate key just in case I ever found myself in this predicament. I tried not to kick myself too hard for forgetting.

"You're way too trusting, Sedona," Callie exclaimed behind me as she cautiously looked about to see if anyone had seen me retrieve the spare. I'd have to find a different hiding spot again.

I turned the key in the handle and entered the bookstore. "You're not the first person to tell me that." My response came out in a grumble, and my friend laughed.

"Then I agree with him. Just don't tell him that." Him being Micah. "Never tell a man that you think he's right. It sets a very dangerous precedent, and they become unbearably arrogant after that." There was a knowing gleam in her eyes that told me she spoke from experience.

"Duly noted." I glanced about. Everything looked normal and the same. I waited for the sensation of dread that often rose up and threatened to suffocate me, but it never came. "I think I'm good now."

And I was.

We exchanged one last hug with the promise to have lunch some time later that week. Watching her leave reminded me of the importance of not completely shutting myself off from the world. That sometimes the risk of letting people in and truly seeing who you are was worth it.

Lifting the sage to my nose, I took in a deep breath.

"Time to clean."

Then, with the lighter I found in the top drawer of the front counter, I got to work smudging away the trauma of the past.

CHAPTER 3

I knew exactly where he'd be, and after successfully smudging every inch, nook, and cranny of the store, I locked up for the second time that day and made my way to him.

Nerves coursed through me as I mentally rehearsed the conversation I was about to have. It was hard not to shrink away from admitting I'd acted like a complete loon. I wasn't used to losing control like that. Trusting that he'd forgive my momentarily lapse in judgment, I walked through the white picket fence gate and trudged up the steps to his door.

Piece of cake, I muttered softly to myself, taking in a fortifying breath of courage. This was what it meant to be a responsible adult. Emotions were often complicated, expressing them sometimes difficult. But that didn't mean a person got a free ticket to act as they wanted and not face the consequences.

This was my walk of shame of sorts. Thankfully the only person who knew how I was feeling right now was securely inside the house, on the other side of the door I was knocking on.

The sound of footsteps heightened my anxiety, and I gulped hard. Without thinking, I slipped my hand into my pocket and found the labradorite crystal I carried. The heat sizzled against my skin, and I smiled with a little more confidence.

Tomorrow I'd send Callie her favorite bottle of wine from Soothing Sips. That or a fresh order of Mexican goodies from Tacos for Daze. I didn't think she realized just how much her small intervention this afternoon had helped. It was the difference between night and day —calm and chaos. Standing there in Eloise's new age store had helped unknot my abilities so I could focus.

The door swung open, and my stomach dipped. Thankfully I didn't gasp out loud like an idiot. I didn't know what had happened, but the sight of Micah standing there in just a plain white T-shirt and dark denim jeans made my heart race a little faster and my mouth water.

I never wanted that feeling to go away.

"Hey," I whispered, a sudden shyness taking over.

He leaned against the door frame, his arms folded across his chest. Someone else might've read his body language as being apprehensive or cautious, but I wasn't paying attention to any of that. My gaze went to his arms and the sight brought back the memories of how safe and secure I'd felt in his embrace. There was nothing intimidating or scary about this man. Even with the knowledge that he was a warrior amongst angels didn't dim or erase that growing attraction between us.

"Hi." A dimple appeared as he offered me a warm smile. God, how I loved making that appear.

"Can we talk?" My request came out rushed, as if the words themselves worried that I wouldn't utter them. "I need to explain." It was tempting to purge everything right there and then to babble and ramble like I was prone to do. I wanted to do this right, however, so I gestured over my shoulder. "It's a nice night. Want to go for a walk with me?"

Micah nodded, and disappeared into the house, no doubt warning Holly that if she dared to step a foot outside the house and the protective warding he'd established, he'd ground her for fifty lifetimes. Right now, that was his favorite threat whenever she was feeling rebellious.

Not that his young charge purposely tested her limits. Austin's attack had scared the bejeezus out of her. She'd also gotten it into her head that she wanted to go to Havenwood Falls High when they had registration for the new school year. It meant she'd have to prove she was reliable and could follow the lengthy list of rules he'd no doubt insist she agree to.

I was silently rooting for her. She was a good kid having to deal with a shitty destiny. It wasn't her fault who her father was or that there was a price out for her death. Details about their life before coming to Havenwood Falls were still elusive and fiercely protected by Micah. He was firm when he said that the less I knew, the better. What I did know was enough to make me worry. I couldn't imagine the pressure of always looking over my shoulder, studying the shadows for a constant threat. It was hard enough dealing with the repercussions of being an empath.

Micah returned, and I stepped aside as he locked the door.

"Can't be too careful, right?" I added, trying to find a way to bridge the conversation from politeness to what was pressing against my heart.

He simply nodded. I didn't like quiet Micah.

"Did you know that flamingos bend their legs at the ankle?" I continued, keeping my tone light and open. "They basically stand on tiptoe." As if to demonstrate, I stood on mine and looked at Micah, hoping against hope that I'd be rewarded with some kind of indication of what he was thinking. When we'd started dating, one of the ground rules had been that I would try not to use my abilities on him without permission. Relationships were about trust, and I'd been adamant that he wouldn't ever have to worry about me trying to gain an unfair advantage. I still remembered that conversation where Aunt Millicent had given it away that she'd asked me to spy on him. The hurt in his eyes and voice was something I never wanted to see again.

"Interesting." It was all he said.

I took that as a good sign.

"Did you know that rollercoasters were invented to distract Americans from sin?" That made his eyebrows raise. I licked my lips and smiled. "Yeah, I think that guy's name was something Thompson." I briefly paused as I searched my memory. "Marco . . . Marcus . . ."

Then it came like a lightning strike. "LaMarcus. That's it. LaMarcus Thompson. It was his way of giving New Yorkers a more wholesome pastime than visiting saloons and brothels." My face reddened. "Not sure why he thought there was a comparison." My cheeks flushed as heat crept over my skin. Now my mind was on sex . . . sex with Micah.

I could tell he was stifling his need to laugh, biting the insides of his mouth. We started walking, side by side, his shoulder brushing against mine.

"I know which one I'd prefer." His answer caused me to stumble, and I reached out to steady myself with his arm. Micah said nothing else. At least he was consistent.

There wasn't really any kind of destination as we strolled down the street, turning at one corner, only to head in a different direction at the next. More facts tumbled about in my head. It wasn't what I wanted to talk about, though. I felt like there was this giant proverbial elephant sitting in the room between us—the memory of my arguing with him earlier.

I bit the bullet before my impatience broke and slapped me hard.

"Micah?" I ignored the way I asked him timidly.

He didn't answer as we rounded another corner, and right as I was about to grab his arm and force him to look at me, he took charge and pulled me into him. No words were exchanged as I peered up into his stormy expression. There wasn't just one emotion simmering within his gaze. I had to force myself to blink before I got swept away in the hurricane.

"I'm so sorry," I uttered, hoping that it wouldn't come across as feeble. I didn't get a chance to add anything else before he crushed his mouth to mine, tightening his embrace around me.

He was kissing me.

He wasn't being silent anymore because the smoldering kiss he was delivering was saying everything for him.

I didn't resist.

I didn't stop him, so we could talk about our feelings and what an idiot I was.

I let his lips press against mine, and when his tongue stroked the seam of my mouth, I opened up completely. The groan that erupted at the first touch of his tongue almost buckled my knees. There was no uncertainty in the way he kissed me or how, with a simple caress of Micah's breath at my throat, he could be so dominant and masterful. This was the kind of kiss that I read about in books—the type that laid claim and laid bare. Micah was telling me that all was forgiven. He was showing me that nothing had changed. He was proving, once and for all, that I wasn't alone . . . that I had him.

I wrapped my arms around his neck, not wanting this moment to end. Not because it would mean I still needed to apologize, but because, just like the crystal in my pocket, it filled me with a delicious heat that made me feel invincible. It filled me with light—one that blasted away the doubt that had been lurking there.

His fingers tangled in my hair, sending chills through my body, prickling my scalp. Everywhere he touched obliterated the worries I had about us. I just couldn't shake the doubt that whispered the attack was my fault.

"Micah," I murmured, barely able to get his name out.

"It doesn't matter," came his response, his own breathing a little ragged. "I believed you that night when you came to stop me from leaving with Holly."

My mind raced to remember. Then suddenly it was there.

"I can't promise what tomorrow holds, but we'll face it together."

I'd meant every word when I'd said it a month ago. In that moment, I'd felt so brave, so unbelievably confident that there was nothing that could stand in our way to happiness. I'd been so naïve.

"Do you still believe that?" Cradling my face between his hands, his thumb brushed back and forth over my cheek. Each caress left shivers in its wake. "Please tell me you still believe it."

Did I?

Did I still feel that conviction, especially in the wake of my suppressed guilt?

I wanted to say yes, but for some reason, I couldn't get it to leave the tip of my tongue.

"But how can you trust me?" It came out so soft that Micah had to lean in to catch my question.

Taking hold of my hands, he brought them to his mouth, kissing the backs of my fingers. "Because I know your heart, Sedona. Because I know you would never wish Holly or me harm." When he saw I was about to argue and push my point further, he brushed the pad of his thumb lightly over my bottom lip before leaning in to feather an even lighter kiss over my mouth. "Sometimes bad things happen. Sometimes they happen despite every precaution taken. All we can do is face each challenge when it comes."

I started to shake my head. "It can't be that simple, though. We're not talking about a small oversight here, Micah. I brought someone into your lives who had every intention of kidnapping Holly. This Collector person is a real and genuine threat. Not some perceived threat. Not some distant phantom wailing and rattling its chains."

"And we thwarted that attempt."

"That bullet could've easily killed her." This was an admission that lay right at the foundation of my guilt. I didn't care that I'd been the one who got shot. My entire focus was on that sweet teenager whom Micah had sacrificed so much to protect and keep hidden.

"Yes, and thankfully, it didn't." He stroked away the single tear that had escaped from my eye. "It wasn't your fault, Sedona."

I lowered my defenses and made myself vulnerable to him. Standing there in the street where the town continued about its nightly business, oblivious to the two people struggling to find a balance in their relationship, I closed my eyes and rested my head against his chest. I could hear his heart beating, and slowly, my own matched it.

"How do you do that?" I asked, not moving.

"Hmm?" His response rumbled against my ear. "Do what?"

"Make things calm while standing in the midst of a storm." I was tempted to sneak a peek at his face, but that would require moving, and I was feeling too comfortable and safe in his embrace. This was all so new to me still.

I felt him shrug. "I don't know. I guess I try to stay as true to myself and what I believe as I can. The love I feel for you is real, so I focus on that."

Butterflies fluttered in my stomach at the sound of him saying he loved me. "You make it sound so easy, though."

He finally laughed, the sound filling the night air. "It's far from easy, but worth the effort. You decide what you give your attention to. I choose the silver linings." His next words thrilled me. "I choose us."

"I didn't mean to lose my temper with you today. I could hear the words coming out of my mouth but did nothing to stop it. I was feeling insecure, and once I started, it came out like verbal diarrhea." I cringed at the last word. Definitely not conducive to talking about love. "You must've thought I was crazy."

His hand was firm at the small of my back, and he added a little pressure there. "Want to know what I thought?"

This time I stepped out of our embrace and really looked into his kind face. There wasn't a trace of annoyance or frustration. His were the features of a man who was being open and honest.

"Yes, please. Makes it easier than guessing."

And getting it wrong, I added mentally.

"I wished I'd known you were carrying such a heavy burden, something that was never yours to begin with." He kept his hands where they'd fallen to his sides, his fingers moving ever so slightly, like he was trying not to reach out and touch me. "I can't change what happened. I felt helpless this afternoon as I watched the dam you've been using to keep everything inside crack and crumble. You were hurting."

"That doesn't excuse me lashing out at you, though, Micah."

He nodded. "It doesn't, but it helps me understand better. Plus, I knew once you calmed down, you'd come so we could talk. Time has a way of healing wounds, Sedona. Space does the same, but I can't seem to keep myself from reaching out and holding you close." And with that last confession, his arms were back around me, and this time I didn't try to step away. I reveled in the warmth from his body.

"So we're good?" I asked, just to make sure.

"We were never not good," he replied. "As long as we can talk through it, we'll be able to get through anything. Just don't shut me out, okay?"

"Right back atcha," I answered, feeling lighter. He laughed at my teasing.

"Let me get you home."

We walked again in comfortable silence, holding hands as the sounds of cars passing by finally filled my ears. I'd basically tuned everything out except us. I hadn't noticed that people were still out and about.

As we reached the end of the street, someone came around the corner, bumping into me as they passed by.

I didn't pay them any attention, my focus still on the miracle that was me and Micah.

We'd overcome another hurdle—this one of my own creation. Unlike my earlier doubt, today had somehow made us stronger as a couple. I could feel it all the way down to my toes. Everything felt . . . right.

And the heated kiss we exchanged at my door just proved the thought that once again floated to the surface.

Life was good.

Love was good.

So very, very good.

CHAPTER 4

ever let somebody's drama determine the outcome of your day.

The desktop calendar of daily quotes was spookily accurate today as I caught sight of the last person I wanted to see this early in the morning.

"Any more words of advice, Mr. Terry Mark?" I asked out loud, staring hard at the square printed paper as though it would magically add an extra quote or two. Unfortunately, magical powers or not, I wasn't Harry Potter talking to Tom Riddle's journal.

Sometime in the future, I was going to need to fix this tension between my aunt and me. As an empath, I got an inside advantage to how she viewed the world—to how she saw our relationship. Buried deep beneath her pride and driving need to be useful lurked her love for me. I couldn't fault her for constantly pushing me toward using my magic more. With no children of her own, she saw it as safeguarding our family's legacy and ensuring that her knowledge didn't fall by the wayside.

What I struggled with was her inability to even acknowledge my own needs. That same thirst for power didn't run through my veins. When ambition was handed out in Heaven, I was busy reading or something, and missed out. She saw it as a character flaw to desperately squash. Once my parents died, and then my grandfather, the pressure fell even harder on her shoulders.

For the most part, we danced around each other, our game of tug of war often ending in mutual frustration.

It didn't help that I antagonized her. I considered it payback for the countless lectures she delivered, her voice droning as she talked about family honor and my lack of respect.

And here she was again, about to grace me with her presence. The look of determination that filled her features didn't betray her purpose for the visit. Neither did the haughty scowl she offered when she entered.

"Good morning, Sedona. I trust that everything is well with you." Her greeting was almost dismissive as she strode past where I was sitting at the counter, her focus directed toward the back of the store.

So she was here for that, I mused. It was going to be *that* kind of social call.

Secreted in the far back wall, beyond the entrance that led to the store room, was a door that led to the upstairs apartment. My grandfather had lived up there until he took his last breath, and it was where the pull-down ladder was kept for the attic.

No one had cause to go up there. Going up to the attic to find some window display inspiration was the last time I'd ventured that way, and honestly, it hurt my heart too much to be surrounded by all the items that represented my beloved grandfather's life.

"What can I help you with you, Auntie?" I asked, forcing her to stop in her tracks and talk with me. If she was wanting into his apartment, she was going for one reason only—the extensive library of magical tomes and paraphernalia he'd collected and inherited.

That I'd inherited, according to his will.

There was no mistaking her exasperation. "I need to find a certain volume from the *family* collection." I didn't miss the heavy emphasis placed on *family*. "Unless you're ready to step up and do your part." A smug smile briefly curled her lips before she returned to her normal expression.

I didn't take the bait. "Wait until I'm finished with this." I gestured to the pile of paperwork I'd been successfully ignoring up until now. "Then I can let you in and get it for you." I threw her one of my own grins, feigning interest in the electricity bills.

"I wouldn't want to rush you, niece." Her foot betrayed her false patience, tapping twice.

I rested my hands on the top of the counter and pushed my chair back. "What were you looking for in particular?"

Part of me really didn't want to ask, because she would see it as a foothold into berating me about my shameful reluctance.

Aunt Millicent was nothing if not predictable. "Important research for the coven." Peering over her glasses so she resembled an eagle looking down on the world, she started speaking the words that began most of the arguments we had. "If you didn't squander your gifts, you would know. The coven is always needing the support of powerful witches like you, Sedona." She even had the same tone of shame and disgust. "You have no idea how embarrassing it is to see others bring their family members into the fold, and yet I remain alone in my duty."

I was careful to keep my own sigh quiet as I continued up the stairs. "Yeah, I imagine it's got to suck."

That was the wrong thing to say. "Sedona Mathews, that's enough of your sarcasm, thank you very much." She grabbed my arm and squeezed harder than anticipated. I squeaked from the brief flash of pain as her nails dug in through my light sweater. When I added a loud *ow*, she finally released her grip. "You know I do this because I love you. I wouldn't push if I didn't recognize what great potential you have. Not just as your birthright, but also because I believe you can achieve anything once you put your mind to it."

This was the closest she ever came to praising me. As with any of our conversations, there was always a major *but* at the end of such small compliments.

"But?" I prompted, wanting to speed this up. I still had bills and applications to ignore.

"Why must you try my patience?" she exclaimed, sounding more and more like she was the victim of some horrible verbal assault. "All

I've ever wanted was to see you succeed, Sedona. Is it wrong for me to want greater things for you?"

So help me, if she sniffled or feigned any kind of emotion, I was going to stop, go back downstairs, and leave the store. I wasn't in the mood for her brand of encouragement.

"Sorry, Aunt Millicent," I mumbled, choosing instead to not add fuel to the flames between us. We finally entered into the small living room area in my grandfather's home. A heavy coating of dust covered every surface, all except for the large pieces of furniture I'd thrown sheets over to protect.

It seemed she had something else to say. "Why do you still keep that tiny apartment over at Havenwood Village when you could easily move into here?" She scrunched up her face as she looked like she was about to sneeze. "I'm sure he would be pleased knowing you were close."

Turning about in the room, I took in all the familiar sights that still pulled at my heart and memories. We spent countless nights sitting in front of the now abandoned fireplace—both he and I with our books opened, a comfortable silence enveloping us as we read. Many discussions had been shared across the small dining room table —some that would cause my aunt's eyebrows to rise so high that they'd fall over the top of her head and down her back. My grandfather always nurtured my love of facts and learning. There was never a topic we couldn't tackle together, and some of my earliest childhood recollections came from the tidbits he shared over a meal with me.

I shrugged, not really knowing how to answer her. It had always been an expectation that one day I'd make the decision and move everything over. It made a ton of sense, considering I worked downstairs. Maybe that was why I hadn't made the leap yet. It was nice having a separation between business and personal.

Besides, the grief I still harbored over the loss of a most beloved patriarch hadn't faded enough for my liking. In the back of my mind, I still held the belief that he was tinkering around while I worked downstairs. I wasn't ready to let go of the fantasy.

I eventually pointed over to the closed door. "Help yourself."

Wrapping my arms around myself tightly, I was ready to just leave her up here to figure it out. "I'll see you back downstairs."

"You're not going to assist?" My reluctance to stay was nothing surprising. Her gaze sharpened as though she could somehow break me by sheer will. Then something completely unexpected happened. I would later wonder if I'd imagined it.

Her facial muscles relaxed, and I caught a small glimpse of whom she might have been.

"Sedona, I know I'm not the most pleasant to be around, but I ask that we put aside our differences long enough so I can find the answers I'm seeking." There was a foreign tone to her plea. It was with a gasp that I realized she was being one hundred percent sincere. "Please."

It was with that same earnestness that I heard myself replying I would.

I hadn't entered my grandfather's magic room since his death, and now I was willingly following my aunt inside.

Hell must've frozen over.

That or the purple pig had sprouted wings and was now circling overhead.

For whatever reason, there was one thought that stuck.

Aunt Millicent had said please.

Holy crap.

"CONSIDER WHAT I SAID CAREFULLY, Sedona. That's all I ask."

To say the past few hours upstairs with my aunt was like visiting the Twilight Zone would have been an understatement. It had been hard to trust the softer side she showed me—that niggly voice in the back of my head warning me that this was some kind of trap intended to manipulate me.

But over the course of three hours, I'd laughed more with my aunt than I could remember ever doing before. I caught myself opening up and sharing some of the memories I had with my grandfather. Where I expected some snide comment or caustic remark, Aunt Millicent was attentive and genuine in her reactions. It was as if some kind of temporal shift had happened, and this was a new reality where we actually got along.

As we walked back downstairs and toward the front door, a sense of regret filled me. I didn't want this visit to end. I actually liked the woman my aunt could be—that is, if she ever stopped nagging me.

So when she turned one last time and asked me to ponder our discussion, that old familiar feeling of frustration flared back into existence. Her new personality had run its course, and today would slip into the shadows again, something I would later count as a fluke.

I nodded reluctantly, already regressing to our old, familiar patterns. "Sure."

Compassion filled her gaze. Maybe I hadn't imagined this afternoon. "Things are stirring up in town, and we all must be prepared. That's another reason why I push you so hard. I want you to have every chance of surviving it." There was a small, sharp inhale as her expression turned to panic. She'd disclosed something she shouldn't have. "You have so much of your mother in you."

I scrunched my forehead. That was a weird subject change.

"She was this stubborn?" I fired back, already knowing the answer.

It was something that my grandfather celebrated, and one of the many character flaws my aunt liked to point out. I always felt a tinge of pride at the reminder that I was my mother's daughter.

There was that look of exasperation I'd been waiting for. With a slight eye roll, Aunt Millicent shook her head like she wasn't quite sure what to do with me. "Yes, but my point was that she failed to accept the power she held and the responsibility she shouldered in wielding it."

I hated that every conversation seemed to devolve into the same argument.

"It's called a choice," I answered, annoyed that after all this time, she still couldn't accept this fundamental truth. "We get to decide what's best for us. What makes us happy. What we want to pursue, and what we'd rather let go of. We decide the priorities and important things in our life."

Gone was the soft undertone from my voice as disappointment followed with the realization that this . . . *this* would always be the relationship we had.

"I never pictured you the coward." Her abrupt judgment felt like a slap in the face.

I swung open the front door and stepped to the side. "And I didn't imagine someone who claimed to love me would actually hurt me." I gestured outside. "I think it's best you leave now."

"You always were overly dramatic. I suppose that's what comes with spending your life with your head in the clouds and nose in a book." She stood in the doorway, peering down her nose at me. "Forgive me for thinking after all you suffered with Austin and the questions your boyfriend keeps asking, you'd be begging for my help in sharpening your abilities." She had the nerve to tut and shake her head like she was the victim here. It was even lower for her to try to manipulate me using Micah and the mysterious Collector.

Micah had said he was trying to find out information about the one I truly held responsible for Austin and the attempt to kidnap Holly.

"Enough," I blurted out as my eyes began filling with tears. "I need you to hear me. I am not the Sedona you have all these expectations for. I'm not some pawn to control. I'm not your doll to dress up and play with. I'm sorry that I'm not this perfect niece that you can show off around the water cooler. I'm sure it's a source of embarrassment, but I am who I am. If you can't accept that—accept me—then maybe it's time we finally end this charade and call it quits."

My chest tightened. My heart ached. I loved my aunt, but there came a point where enough was enough.

"Confidence. That's all you're lacking."

The sense of utter letdown was suffocating. She hadn't listened to a single word.

"Good night, Millicent." Closing the door on her, I slid the lock into place, and turned around with my back against the frame. Tears streamed down my cheeks. My body felt as though I'd just been hit by a freight train, exhaustion setting in.

I don't know how long I stood there quietly crying. At some point I felt Maxwell appear and saw him from the corner of my eye, but then he disappeared. I was grateful for the ghost's reluctance in finding out what was wrong, because I still had no idea of the right way to explain the rollercoaster of emotions I was going through.

How could I say out loud that I would never be anything more than a tool to be used by the only immediate family I had in town?

How could I acknowledge the truth that I'd kept buried inside— that even after all the many hurtful actions and comments, I still harbored the secret desire to one day be a true family?

This last discussion had shattered that fragile hope I'd somehow managed to keep protected all these years. It was time to grow up and face reality.

It was time to let go.

CHAPTER 5

*J*f it wasn't for the fact that I knew Havenwood Falls wasn't capable of insanely hot temperatures, I would've bet my life I was experiencing a heat wave. It had started when I'd peeled off my sheets and comforter this morning and had steamrolled through my day until I was forced to resort to using a spray bottle filled with the iciest, coldest water I could find.

The temptation to run upstairs and stand in front of the freezer was crippling, and as another trickle of sweat rolled down the center of my back, it was everything I could do not to yell out that the bookstore was closed.

It was stifling and unbearable.

It was also embarrassing, because nobody else had any idea what I was carrying on about. Micah's thick flannel shirt made me want to shred the garment from his body. He was wearing too much, and just the sight of him made me feel claustrophobic in my own skin.

I spritzed myself again.

And again.

Damn, it was nauseatingly hot.

"Maybe I should take you to the doctor?" Micah asked, for what felt like the millionth time. It didn't matter that he could heal me with a mere touch of his hand. He'd declared the thermometer I'd stashed in the first aid kit was faulty, even as the tiny display screen revealed that I wasn't running a fever.

"Other than the heat, I feel fine." I plastered a smile across my face like it would convince him. "Why waste the doctor's time if it's just a twenty-four-hour thing?"

"Perhaps you're going through the change," Maxwell announced, choosing this moment to appear. "Although you are a tad too young to be affected by such a malady."

I wanted to throttle the ghost for even suggesting it. "This isn't menopause, you ill-mannered pain in my butt!"

If it was even possible, I felt my cheeks grow hotter. I pressed my hands against my warm skin. That was the other conundrum.

I was hot from the inside, but normal to the touch.

Micah reached out and felt my forehead for himself. "I don't like this," he murmured. "Maybe you should go home and rest. I can watch over things here if you're worried about the store."

While lying about on the couch with a book in my hand seemed heavenly and inviting, my extra-long to-do list wouldn't allow it.

"Which brings me to the real reason why I asked you to come today." This next part was exciting, and I couldn't help the butterfly feeling in my stomach. New things and projects always gave me a good case of nervous jitters. I picked up the top piece of paper from the flyers I'd just finished printing out.

I held it up to show him and Maxwell. "What do you think?"

Micah's eyes moved back and forth as he silently read the information. "You want to host a book swap here at the store?"

My nod was a little too enthusiastic, but I didn't try to curb it. I couldn't help my passion for reading.

"Yep, well, actually out in the street, but yeah. I've already gotten the town council's approval, and I know it's short notice—" I paused as panic rose up my throat mid-sentence. When the idea had come to me early this morning while I was showering, I'd worried that three days wasn't enough time to make arrangements and organize the event. It wasn't until everything started falling into place that I gave myself permission to believe. Hopefully, it would be the first of many.

"It is, but I have faith you can do it, my sweet girl." Maxwell had tossed aside his usual sarcastic comments, and instead wore a look of pride. "Give you something else to focus on besides that witch whom I won't mention." For someone I'd only really known for the past few years since I started running Shelf Indulgence, Maxwell was fiercely protective when it counted. Phantom tears had filled his own eyes when I'd entered this morning. He'd heard it all last night, and it had pained him to witness it. "You've got this one to help as well, although I don't think he can hear me." So far, Micah hadn't acted like he saw the resident spook. I didn't bother questioning it. Their relationship was an odd one.

"The ghost is right," Micah added, finally acknowledging him.

"Ooooh, so he does see me!" That seemed to put the proverbial firecracker beneath Maxwell as his ghostly eyes flashed brightly.

For the first time today, Micah turned to where Maxwell was standing with a smirk. "I have no problem seeing you. I just choose not to."

I burst out laughing, which in turn made the guys smile wider.

"Play nice." I reached out and slapped Micah across the chest. The movement caused a ripple of desire to flood my body. He was like a walking contradiction—he was all muscles and hardness, his physique in what could only be described as glorious shape. But I'd also experienced what others might consider the polar opposite—in his arms, I could feel the softness of those same muscles as he wrapped me up in his protective embrace.

Soft and hard.

My gaze dropped for a moment as the word *hard* echoed and bounced around inside my brain. It wasn't the first time my thoughts went to a slightly more intimate place. There was so much about Micah I didn't know about yet, but there was one thing I was pretty certain about.

I was excited to explore new possibilities with him.

I'm ready to explore him, came my low, lustful voice.

"So you want me to go hand these out and spread the word?" He had no idea that I'd been quietly undressing him in my mind. That ignorance made me blush, making me wonder if I'd ever be brave enough to act on my inner brazenness. We'd had some pretty intense make-out sessions, but Micah had wanted to take things slowly.

His request had all but blown my mind. Usually I was the one throwing on the brakes when the guys I dated headed straight to the bedroom. The fact that he was the one to slow it down simply intrigued me more. He was different. I loved that about him.

I quickly nodded when I realized they were both waiting for my answer. "Yes, please. The sooner people know, the better I can breathe and stop telling myself I'm crazy for doing it."

Micah read over the flyer again. "You worry too much. I think this is an awesome thing, and after you work your magic, it'll go perfectly." He grabbed my hand and squeezed it. "Plus, maybe it'll clear up some space for new inventory."

This time I did know my cheeks reddened. I wasn't used to someone being that attentive and remembering random outbursts and comments I made. I'd said some off-the-cuff thing about wanting to bring in a whole new collection of books and updating the store's online catalog. Of course, Micah would remember and bring it up right when I needed to hear it.

I refused to let his hand go. "That's the hope." That's when a pang of sadness returned, and I cast a sidelong glance at the applications I'd been ignoring. "I shouldn't have procrastinated. If all goes well, this place will be too busy for just one person." When Maxwell cleared his throat, I added, "And ghost." He winked his gratitude at finally being included.

"Actually, that's the perfect segue into something I wanted to run by you." Micah was doing his best impersonation of the Cheshire Cat. "How would you feel if Holly took over Austin's position?"

It was so not what I thought he would ask.

"I've thought about it too many times to count and disregarded it, because I know how cautious you are with her. Why?" I zeroed in on him and studied his body language. Just out of curiosity, I reached out with my empathic skills to see what he was feeling. Nothing. Even here, alone, he wouldn't—couldn't—lower his guard.

He caught me in the act. "Ask me, Sedona. Don't try to sneak it out of me."

There was enough of a hint of amusement in his voice that I knew he wasn't too mad at my being nosy.

"I'd hire her in a heartbeat, Micah, but I honestly can't have you standing in the corner, or stalking customers throughout the store because Holly is helping them. How many books do you think we'll sell if people don't want to come anymore?" I narrowed my gaze at him. "Be honest. As much as I love having you here, your bodyguard warrior mojo façade will only make her uncomfortable."

Squeezing his hand again, I finally let it go.

I expected Micah to argue with me. Instead, he smiled even bigger. The look he wore rivaled even the happiest child on Christmas morning. You'd have thought he'd just met Santa.

"I found the perfect compromise. A way that Holly can get a tiny taste of independence." There was the guardian I knew. "And you can rest easier knowing that you can toss those resumes in the trash. In fact, let me do that for you." With one swift swipe of his hand, Micah snatched up the pile, and with a grand flourish, deposited them into the bin.

I hated being the Debbie Downer. I didn't always look at the negative, but life had thrown some pretty painful curveballs lately. I was trying not to be too naïve. "Problem solved, huh? Just like that."

His excitement was contagious. It made me want to take his face between my hands and kiss him senseless. His aura glowed brightly— the golden light shining in the flecks of his eyes.

"Maxwell!" Micah all but boomed out his name. "How would you feel about doing a special job for me?"

Again, my boyfriend surprised me. He wanted a ghost to babysit Holly? A being that had no corporeal body and had only recently managed to leave the store.

I was glad to see I wasn't the only one shocked. "While I'm flattered, Micah, I do believe I'm the wrong person for the job." He'd understood the meaning as well.

Micah looked like he couldn't be so easily dissuaded. "I know it sounds crazy, but hear me out. I wouldn't be suggesting this if I didn't believe one hundred percent that it was a viable option. Maxwell," he turned to the older gentleman, "you have your own special bond with Holly, so I believe you will always put her first. She spends most of her time here or at home. As much as I have loved being here and helping, there's going to come a time when I can't. It makes sense."

He now turned his attention to me. "Wouldn't you like to go on a date or spend time alone together? I know how fond you are of Holly, but I also know you want to be wooed and romanced."

Yet another example of him listening to me. I was always telling him about the stories I was reading, swooning over the main characters and their happily-ever-afters.

"True," I agreed tentatively. "I won't lie and say it wouldn't be nice, but never at the expense of Holly and her safety. You're not the only one who takes mental notes. You've made it crystal clear that our relationship can't ever overshadow your main priority of hiding her." There was no resentment in my tone.

"Do you trust me?" For the briefest second, I got a flash of Aladdin offering his outstretched hand to Jasmine. He wanted to show her the world. Micah was asking me to consider the one he was trying to create—a world where he could see a way to both have his cake and eat it, too.

I didn't hesitate. "Absolutely."

"Then let's try this. I wouldn't have suggested this if I hadn't already played out every possible scenario in my head." Maxwell and I still weren't completely convinced. "Fine. Test me."

"What if someone comes in here and has a gun?" It wasn't a hard thing to imagine. There was no point dodging the truth. This had happened.

Micah grimaced. It was still a fresh pain for him as well. "Then you will work your magic, and Maxwell will come for me immediately."

"What if that person leaves with Holly?" It was the ghost's turn to ask.

We continued to grill him for another five minutes, and each time we asked a new question, he came back with a solid answer. This wasn't just some random plan. Micah had given it a lot of thought.

"I can't believe I'm having to convince you about this." He laughed, shaking his head.

"And I can't believe you're willing to loosen that tight grip you've had when it comes to her well-being," I countered.

"Then let's take it day by day. On a trial basis." All humor drained from his face as Micah turned serious. "Trust me. This is the only solution."

He then turned back to Maxwell. "What do you say?"

The ghost studied him thoroughly. Seconds ticked by, and I wondered if Micah could feel the specter's scrutiny clear down to the soles of his feet.

Maxwell fiddled with the end of his moustache, deep in thought.

"Well?" The whole idea was contingent on his agreement.

"If it means I don't have to witness any more of your groping and kissing around here, I say why not." Beneath the fake expression of disgust rose a happier one. He was glad to see me happy and making plans again.

"I'll take that as a yes, Maxwell," Micah said, and he picked up the pile of flyers. "If there's nothing else, I'd better get started on these. I'll have Holly help while I explain the new arrangement."

We all looked over toward the far-right corner of the store. Shelves and displays hid her from our view, but Holly had headed in that direction when they first entered the store. She had no doubt tuned out the world, escaping into the book she'd been carrying.

"Before you go," I blurted, coughing when I heard how weird I sounded. "There's something I need from the attic." I pointed to the ceiling like the gesture would reveal my intention. Or like they needed to know where it was. I was nervous.

Micah nodded. "Then let me know what it is, and I'll grab it for you. Who knows how long these will take to distribute." Rolling the stack into a loose tube, he followed behind me. Any excuse to check out my butt.

The second I heard the door leading upstairs close behind us, I whipped around, and launched myself at Micah. My arms worked their way around his neck, and the kiss I'd been daydreaming about happened.

The flyers dropped to the floor, forgotten, as Micah returned my urgency with that of his own. He didn't hold back. He didn't try to take over or control the aching desire that seemed to explode out from me.

I couldn't get enough of him.

His touch.

His taste.

The sound he made—that guttural groan that just screamed sex.

Everything about my angel was intoxicating, overwhelming, and unbelievably addicting.

I'd told him that once—that he was like that first sip of coffee in the morning, that first chapter in a book that reaches out and whisks you away on an adventure. Books often described it like a drug, but I'd never experienced that. All I knew—all that I was familiar with—was the way his energy set my own on fire. I couldn't keep my own moans from passing through my lips, and some were there simply because I couldn't bear for the kiss to end.

I wanted him.

Wanted all of him.

Right here.

Right now.

My hands dropped to his belt like they'd been doing it forever. There was no feeling awkward or shy. This was where we usually stopped, but I was tired of waiting. Suddenly, I didn't care that we were dangerously close to having our first time in a narrow stairway.

The only thing I could think, that flashed over and over in my mind, was how good this felt, and how natural the next step was. I was by no means a virgin. But these emotions that Micah stirred up in me were definitely new.

The thought made my fingers tremble and slip. His belt was proving to be an obstacle.

Unfortunately, it was enough of a slip that Micah took hold of my hand to stop me.

His breath came out ragged. "Wait."

I stopped and watched as he wet his lips. God, I needed to kiss those lips.

"Why now?" he asked.

"I don't know," I whispered. "It just feels like the right thing to do."

He took my face between his hands and brought his mouth to my forehead, kissing it ever so lightly. "Heaven knows I want this, Sedona."

I tried not to laugh at his choice of words.

It was my turn to sigh as my heart thundered in my chest. I was positively thrumming with desire. It was both terrifying and exhilarating. "So let's take that next step." I peered up into his blue eyes. "I'm ready."

He brushed his thumbs across my cheeks. "Then not like this. I don't want this to be our first time."

Reality crashed around me, and I finally laughed. What the hell had just come over me?

"How about you come over tonight? I'll cook us some dinner, and we'll take it from there." I rose up on my tiptoes and briefly pressed my lips against his. He held my head in place, deepening the kiss until I was back to being aware of only the two of us. I could see why falling in love could be dangerous for empaths. I wasn't just feeling my own emotions. For microbursts of time, I caught his. It was like trying to snatch sparks of light from the air. Just when you think you've captured one, you open your hand and your palm is empty.

I could also see why Micah worried about becoming involved with me. It required a level of trust he wasn't used to. In order to focus on me, he ran the risk of blocking out his focus on Holly. It was enough to make me want to pull back and break the kiss.

If I could.

If I had some kind of choice—my heart overruled my brain this time, willing to drown in desire and excitement.

Micah was the one to do it. "I'd better go." He didn't move, though. It was as if he didn't want to break the magic of the moment either. "Any minute now."

My arms began to drop from where I'd had them around his neck again. Placing my hands on his chest, it was safe to say I'd never been so torn in my life. All it would take was a word, and a few more steps up into the apartment, and it would happen. Micah and I would have sex, and it would be everything I'd ever imagined it to be.

Sometimes being responsible sucked.

I created some much needed distance between our bodies.

"Go. The sooner we get done, the sooner we can start our evening." My voice sounded so needy and guttural. Micah's eyes widened. He liked what he heard.

"I'll let Maxwell know our new plans." He took a step back as well, bumping into the door at the bottom. "Well, not all our plans, but that he'll be watching Holly tonight at my house. I've got plenty of wards there to keep them both safe until I show up."

"Are you sure?" A new wave of concern blasted the last of my desire.

Micah bounded up to where I still stood. He kissed me again, hard and fast. "Positive." He didn't wait for my response. With a wave over his shoulder, he exited through the door. I didn't follow.

Instead I sat on the step, gingerly touching my swollen lips.

Tonight, then.

Tonight, everything would change.

CHAPTER 6

*Y*ou could cut the sexual tension with a knife.

Never in my life had I experienced this intensity personally, making me wonder how I'd ever lived without it. I knew that sounded cheesy, but it took everything I had to breathe through the emotions that filled the air. It had nothing to do with being bombarded with other people's lust and desire.

No, the sensations that were wreaking havoc over my psyche were emanating from me. Part of me wanted to ask Micah if he was drowning in it as well, but every time the words formed in my mouth, I chickened out.

Dinner was almost ready, and the mouthwatering aroma coming from my oven was one of my favorites. I made a mean lasagna when I felt inspired, and staring at Micah as he sat on the other side of my kitchen island had been all the motivation I needed. I wanted to impress him with my culinary skills.

Heck, those were just a few of the skills I was hoping to show him by the end of the night. Wringing my hands in front of me as I studied the timer, I just hoped I didn't let my nerves get the better of me.

Be confident! I inwardly cheered. *It's not like it's rocket science.*

That was the thing, though. It might not be as technical, but with my heart invested, it could end up being just as complicated. I didn't want to wake up tomorrow morning with a heavy dose of regret because we really did make better friends than a couple. Sex wasn't everything, but it was. At least it felt like that right now.

"You're quiet again," Micah said. He'd lit the candles I had gotten out for tonight. The flames flickered against his skin, lighting him up from beneath with a glow that made it impossible to deny. Of course, he was an angel. It should've been obvious from the beginning, if I hadn't been so hung up on how attractive he looked. Maybe it was because I'd been granted a closer look—a sort of peek behind the curtain—that I could truly see his aura.

It was gorgeous.

He was gorgeous.

"You're making me nervous now, Sedona." His voice was soft and gentle. Micah hadn't taken his gaze away from me. "If you're having second thoughts, then all we'll do tonight is eat."

I gulped a little too loudly, drawing attention to my nerves. It wasn't that I was questioning our decision. At least, not like he was thinking. Part of me knew that once we crossed this bridge, there would be no going back. Everything would change. It would be harder to untangle from each other if something went wrong.

"You're not worried?" I asked, grateful for the distraction when the oven's alarm sounded. Grabbing two oven mitts, I carefully removed the hot casserole dish and placed it over the burner to cool off. I didn't see his face when he answered, but I almost lost my grip on the kitchenware at the last minute.

"About us having sex?"

His response shattered any anxiety I'd been wallowing in. When I turned about, it was to find him sitting there, the picture of innocence. It was his cheeky grin that gave him away. He'd done it on purpose.

"No," I laughed, realizing that I hadn't been clear about where my thoughts had strayed. "I'm not worried about *that*." Without thinking, my gaze dropped down the front of his body, resting just below his belt buckle. I had no doubt that tonight would be every bit as magical as I imagined. I just couldn't shake the feeling that by lowering our guard, there was a risk of something bad happening. "I meant us leaving Holly with Maxwell so we could be alone."

Sliding the spatula around the edges of the lasagna, loosening the burned parts from the pan, I immediately felt a new emotion settle in the air. It was the one I best associated with Micah and called his "no nonsense" energy.

"I trust them both to follow my orders." There was a slight twitch in his left eye that gave the truth away.

"How many times have you called Holly or texted her?" Dinner was momentarily forgotten while I leaned across the island to stare deep into his eyes. He couldn't lie to me then. There was no way he was this calm, not after I'd seen some of his past reactions.

His gaze dropped to his phone that was beside him on the countertop. The screen was face down, and I wondered if it was because he didn't want me to see that he was troubled.

"Um," he answered slowly. He leaned in as though he was about to expose some dark secret. I did the same until our faces were mere inches apart. "I plead the fifth." And with a smugness that shot licks of heat down my front until it pooled between my legs, Micah crossed his arms across his chest and sat back.

"Are you even American?" I retorted, slapping my hand down on the island's granite surface. "As an angel, aren't you meant to encompass all of mankind?"

He simply nodded. "Something like that."

His gaze followed me as I began pulling plates out so we could eat. I could feel it—hot and driven—as if he was memorizing every move and nuance.

God help us. How are we going to survive dinner?

"You disappeared again." Sure enough, I'd stopped mid-dishing out the lasagna and been standing there like an idiot, daydreaming. "You do that a lot."

"I do?"

Micah reached out and with the top of his finger, wiped a few drops of the marinara sauce from the plate I'd placed in from of him.

"You get this faraway look. I often feel guilty for speaking up, because you look so content."

I rolled my eyes, handing him a fork. After quickly filling my own plate with a smaller slice of lasagna and a healthier serving of green salad, I came around the island, so I could sit on the stool beside him. "I'm not that bad. I just sometimes get distracted and squirrel."

"Squirrel?"

I loved it when I used words in a way he'd never heard before. "It means that my attention can split easy. One minute I'll be scrolling through a publishing house catalogue, and the next, I'm ten pages deep on Pinterest, searching for finger puppet patterns." That was the best way to describe it. "And it all depends on the day and what's going on. It used to make my grandfather laugh and tease me. I would come into the store when I worked part time there after school and find acorns by my name badge, or on the plate of cookies he left out. It was our own personal joke."

"Because squirrels like nuts."

"And my grandfather had a soft spot for squirrels." I felt sheepish for sharing such a personal memory with him, but it also felt right. This was what normal couples did. I wanted us to be that—regular, normal, reliable, predictable. No drama meant that the chemistry that continually built between us couldn't come to an end.

"I'm quite partial to them, too." The tone in his voice had deepened. Micah was no longer playing with his food, using his fork to push the cucumber drizzled with ranch dressing back and forth through the pasta sauce.

He was looking at me so intently that the odd feeling came back— the one where my surroundings started to grow hazy as my focus on Micah became brutally sharp and clear. He was all I saw. He filled my vision.

"Micah," I murmured, not completely sure what I was trying to say. My mouth opened slightly. I closed it back up.

He caressed the side of my face before tracing the outline of my lips. "What do you need?"

He searched my eyes for some indication of where my head was. I was done thinking about it—fantasizing about it. I was a grown woman, and there was nothing wrong with confessing my wants. No, my needs.

I turned in my seat and placed my hands on his upper thighs. The jeans he was wearing were a frustrating barrier keeping me from what I wanted—to feel his bare skin. To be able to feel him all over. I wasn't sure where these new brazen urges came from, but for just once, I didn't try to rationalize them away.

"You. I need you."

He had the decency to not tease me in return.

He slowly rose to his feet, pushing the stool away with the backs of his legs. Extending his hand to me, he helped me up to join him. Up close and personal, he smelled so good, and without thinking, I buried my face into his chest and inhaled deeply. My hands fisted up in his shirt.

It was getting harder to think clearly.

I wasn't complaining.

"Hold on." In a move that rivaled those in the romantic comedies, Micah scooped me up in his arms, and carried me to my bedroom. He kicked the door closed, and then with an endearing tenderness, he carefully lay me down.

"No one's going to walk in on us, Micah," I joked, the idea of someone watching not altogether unwelcome. "We're completely alone." I sat up and rested back on my hands. "Just you and me."

His smirk was sexy as hell. "And Lavender. I don't want any surprises, so she can hate me later for evicting her from her favorite spot. She can deal with sleeping on the couch tonight." There was that streak of humor he had that always left me feeling good.

Then it hit me.

He was nervous.

The jokes and trying to lighten the mood were his own attempts to keep calm.

That made him even sexier for trying.

"I'm sure she'll understand." I scooted forward until I was at the end of the bed, sitting in front of him. I stroked the sides of his legs before resting my hands at his belt. As I slowly unbuckled it, Micah's breath hitched with each sharp tug I gave. When his belt finally gave way and I'd popped the top button, my finger slowly traced over the zipper's teeth.

He groaned with impatience.

I was surprised I wasn't wanting to rush things either. This moment was all I'd been thinking about, and now . . . now it was going to become a reality.

The zipper made a slight noise as I lowered it.

With a quick jerk, Micah's jeans dropped to his ankles. Seconds later they were kicked across the room. His shirt then joined it in a crumpled pile, leaving him naked. In front of me. Boldly. Proudly.

"Sedona." My name came out husky and raw. He'd asked me what I'd needed earlier, and it was clear to me now exactly what he was needing. The feelings were mutual.

He fingered the neckline of my top, showing incredible control because he hadn't already ripped it from me. I didn't need to read him to know that's what he was thinking. His desires were plastered across his face, revealed in the way he bit his lower lip. His hands trembled a little.

He made me feel fragile. He hadn't even touched me, and already I felt precious to him.

"Let me," I offered, and then, pushing him back so we could swap places, I shoved him on top of the bed. I had an idea, and tonight was already full of magic. It was the kind of night where nothing was impossible, and there was no fear of crashing if you chose to free fall into the moment. It made me brave.

I was the center of his attention, and I reveled in it. I savored how good his gaze felt on my body, how easy it was to imagine his hands touching me everywhere.

First, I inched out of my skirt, holding it up before dropping it to the floor.

Next, I removed my new favorite shirt. It was so silky, and it had felt delicious against my skin all day—like a lover's caress. I tried not to shiver when I felt his breath blow gently against my hip. I tried not to crumble as he followed up with his tongue—the maddening swirling pattern he made enough to snap my patience.

His finger looped under the side of my panties, pulling them down so he could kiss where they'd been. I was a riot of emotions—each one battering against my resolve to savor our first time together. I wanted it to be tender, slow, romantic.

Instead, all I could focus on was the desperation building. I didn't know how long I could hold out, especially as Micah's mouth moved. My knees buckled, and I toppled forward, landing squarely on top of him. My mind instantly recognized the hardness pressed against me.

"I need you in me." I hadn't meant to say it out loud. I rocked my body gently, watching to see how he would react. "Now."

I didn't waste any more time getting undressed, tossing my panties and bra in some direction. All I could see was Micah, the hunger in his eyes, and how ready he was for this to happen. Somehow, while watching me get naked, he'd managed to find a condom.

When he went to get up, I shook my head, my hair loose around my shoulders. "Do you trust me?"

He gestured for me to continue, and I pushed him back until we were both spread out across my bed. I felt an odd sense of satisfaction and pride seeing him there surrounded by my pillows and bedding. He belonged here with me. Fate or not, there was no denying the rightness of the moment.

As I slowly guided him, sliding down his length until he filled me, something clicked inside me. Like a door unlocking after finding its key. There was nothing left to think or feel. All that existed was the desperate need to move.

Micah's hand spanned my waist, holding me as we both found the tempo that curled my toes and had him uttering my name over and over. Suddenly I couldn't wait. I was done keeping that maddening pace, and as I flicked my hips forward, I picked up the speed, and deepened the stroke.

Micah's eyes rolled back right before I couldn't hold his gaze. Thrusting. Rocking. I gripped on tightly before throwing myself forward and collapsing on his chest. The orgasm that ripped through me was unlike any I'd ever experienced—even the ones I gave myself. What made it even more excruciatingly blissful was the sound Micah made the instant he had his own release.

With ragged breath and heaving chests, we clung to each other, and for the smallest of moments, I felt him—Micah with no protective barrier to hide behind. He'd lowered his guard. There was no telling whether it was by accident or intentionally. I basked in the light that radiated from deep inside him.

I'd said he was beautiful. God, what an understatement that was. He was Divine.

We lay like that for a while in silence.

Our bodies were pressed together, yet neither of us moved. Instead, our eyes locked. It was incredibly intimate and vulnerable. It was as if with each breath we took, we bled more into each other, the boundaries between our auras blurring until there was no longer two but one.

If I hadn't believed in magic before, I did now.

When a small voice finally broke the quietness of my mind, I didn't argue. I simply obeyed.

"Micah?"

His breathing had steadied to the point I thought he'd started falling asleep. The crispness of his response told me he was far from that. "Yeah?"

"Again."

The night had only just begun.

CHAPTER 7

$\mathcal{I}$ stared at myself in the mirror.

Nope, I was still Sedona Mathews.

I'd had sex before, so being with Micah hadn't "popped my cherry," so to speak, but as I peered closer over the vanity cabinet, I half expected to be glowing . . . or different . . . or someone else.

Because while I'd had good sex in the past, that wasn't how I would define last night.

That hadn't just been great sex—it had been phenomenal.

Every single cell in my body still vibrated quietly as if they were basking in the sweet afterglow. I hadn't been able to stop smiling, and there was definitely a twinkle in my eye.

The hot shower I'd just enjoyed had done wonders on my sore muscles, and I couldn't quite decide if I was happy not to limp today or not. I kind of liked having the reminder that my world had been thoroughly rocked.

And I'd held my own.

In fact, there had been a point where I'd taken over, surprising even myself by claiming exactly what my body demanded. For an angel, Micah hadn't blinked an eye. There was nothing saintly about the way he'd worshiped my body, and I would've sold my soul to the Devil himself to keep Micah working that magic with his mouth.

While I hadn't woken up with birds chirping and woodland creatures surrounding my bed, there was a pep in my step as I finished dressing, grabbed the last slice of toast I'd made, and headed out the door.

I felt different.

I felt new.

I felt . . . incredibly . . . horny. I couldn't remember the last time I'd actually physically hungered after someone else. The craving was so strong that I was all but running toward the store, hoping that Micah would drop by before running his errands.

I was already calculating the time it would take me to arrive and whether or not I could open the store up a few hours late, when I bumped into Callie coming out of her consignment store. Fortune was shining down on us, because it was the first time I'd seen her without a coffee in her hand this early in the day. I liked to tease her that she was a "double fister," and that one day she'd get in trouble carrying two hot items in her hands. That had earned me a smirk and a muffled response that was dirty and gutter-worthy.

I'd blushed back then, but now as the memory rose, I wondered what the logistics would be to perform it. The image in my head was enough to scandalize the morality of even the most liberal members in Havenwood Falls.

"Whoa, Sedona!" my friend exclaimed, instantly reaching out to steady herself. "Where's the fire?"

In my pants! I wanted to reply. It was honestly on the tip of my tongue, and by some miracle, I managed to stifle the urge to blurt it.

Callie gave me a quick once over, that look that told me she was trying to assess the situation with her own gypsy-demon gifts. If I thought life was tough as an empath, I knew it was equally sucky for her. She saw things—often events she'd rather be ignorant about—and people weren't always receptive to being told their secrets.

Where I let their judgments hurt me, Callie shrugged it off. That's what made her so badass in my eyes.

"Sorry." I laughed, doing my best to convince her I wasn't crazy.

She hadn't stopped studying me, and it wasn't until a huge grin spread across her face that I realized she knew.

Maybe I was wearing a massive neon sign over the top of my head that flashed: *I had amazing sex last night! Woohoo!*

Callie didn't warn me. She tugged sharply on my arm, with the forceful "get in here now" command that I knew better not to ignore. Her grin was contagious, and when she shoved her finger right in front of my nose, I knew I was in for it.

"Explain yourself, Sedona Mathews. Right now." She folded her arms across her chest. "I mean it."

I decided to feign ignorance. "I'm sooo-oorry?" I drew out, pretending not to know what she meant. "I wasn't paying attention to where I was going. I'm running late." I added that last bit as an afterthought.

"Baaaah." She cupped her hands around her mouth and made a loud, obnoxious noise. "Wrong. Try again."

I tilted my head to the side. "Um?"

She poked my chest this time. "You. Had. Sex. Which means . . . You. Had. Sex. With. Micah." She used her finger to add extra emphasis. Not once did she let me look away. "Go ahead and try to deny it." There was that smug grin again. She knew.

"Well . . ." I was having fun drawing out my confession. I was filled with relief that she'd stopped me, because I was desperate to tell someone about it. The longer it bounced about in my head, the easier it would be to convince myself it was merely a dream. "If you want to know the truth . . ."

Excitement flared in her eyes. "Wait!" Then, after dragging me through the store, she gestured for me to sit in one of the chairs while she grabbed her cup of coffee. "Okay. Now spill the beans!"

I picked at the hole beginning to form at the knee of my jeans. "Did you know that if you're having a hard time orgasming, it might be because your feet are cold. Put on some socks and see if it helps."

Callie sprayed the mouthful of coffee she'd just taken all over.

"Sedona," she blurted, unsure of where to wipe first. Using the cuffs of her sweater, Callie swiped the soft fabric across her mouth first. With an annoyed look, she tossed a cloth to me. "What the hell?"

I kept up the pretense and gave a nonchalant shrug. "I read it somewhere and figured it was my civic duty to pass that helpful nugget of knowledge on."

It was my turn to study my friend. Right as she moved to take another sip from her ceramic mug, I let another truth bomb slip.

"Also, did you know latex condoms are made with a milk protein? Do you think this means vegans can't use them?" I tried to wear the most innocent expression I could muster, but as her eyes grew wide and she almost choked, I couldn't hold it a second longer.

I burst into laughter and threw the cloth back at her.

Callie was speechless. She kept staring at me like I'd suddenly grown two or three heads. I didn't flinch when she lashed out, grabbed my arms, and gently shook me. "Who are you? And what have you done to my sweet friend?"

I felt her magic brush up against my aura. She honestly thought something was wrong with me.

"It's me, silly," I answered, the muscles in my stomach sore from laughing so hard. "I was just messing with you." I still hadn't confessed the truth about Micah, but right as I went to, something else caught my eye. "Oh. My. God. When did that come in?"

I slid off the chair and grabbed the metal hanger on the clothes rack. It was as if the heavens had opened and set a spotlight on the most beautiful dress I'd ever seen.

If it could even be classified as a dress. It was definitely the most risqué thing I'd ever considered buying. Usually, I would look wistfully at such items and immediately talk myself out of adding it to my conservative wardrobe. While I didn't wear pant suits and such, this showed more skin than even my bathing suit.

It was perfect.

"I'm trying this on!" I announced, and without waiting for Callie to argue that I was still ignoring her most pressing question, I headed toward the fitting room. I was already stripped off and stepping into the black, tiny, stretchy dress by the time I heard her outside.

"Sedona?" She sounded hesitant now. "Is everything okay?" I could almost imagine her biting her bottom lip as she fielded my response. "You don't seem like yourself."

That made me scrunch my brow and temporarily forget why I was in the small enclosure. "I'm who I've always been. I'm still me."

I glanced back at the floor length mirror.

Was I really different now?

Had being with Micah really changed who I was?

Did it matter?

Poking my head through the door, I flashed her a happy grin. "Unless you're referring to the mind-blowing sex I had last night."

And with that, I promptly closed the door and waited for the explosion.

Callie all but kicked the door open and stood with her hands firmly on her hips. "You brat! How long were you going to string me along, Miss Casually-Drops-The-Truth-Like-It-Was-Nothing?"

I could see her warring emotions clearly: excitement for me, annoyance at my teasing, curiosity about what I thought, and a healthy dose of disbelief. The last time we'd even touched the topic of when my first time with Micah would be, I'd neatly sidestepped it.

"You can't blame me for the ruse. It's too much fun teasing you." I'd seen all that I needed with the dress. It fit like a silken glove and would feel incredible if I wore it without any underwear. Perhaps I'd model it for Micah later. The idea made my insides heat and smolder. "I'm going to buy this now."

She nodded.

To show her I hadn't meant to deceive her, I gave her a tight hug. "It was beyond anything I'd ever hoped for."

There was a wonder that colored my words—an amazement that revealed how I truly felt. I was still needing to pinch myself.

"Is it true what they say about angels?" Callie wiggled her brows at me suggestively.

My nod was filled with enthusiasm. "Absolutely."

We were back by the cash register, and Callie was folding the dress to drop into a bag. "Really? I always wondered."

I did a quick look over my shoulder to make sure there weren't any customers lurking too closely to overhear us. Even though the store had only just opened, I was still surprised to see I was the only one in here. Most of us knew if we wanted to find a great deal, we needed to get here first thing in the morning.

"The bigger the hands . . ." I held mine up and wiggled my fingers. "The bigger the wings!"

She slapped me hard. I deserved it. Callie was one of the few people who knew about Micah. While I hadn't confided why he'd brought Holly to Havenwood Falls, I had sworn her to secrecy about him being an angel. As much as I loved having Maxwell as a confidant, it had been a godsend becoming close friends with Callie.

After paying and getting everything squared away, I finally owned up to the real reason I'd bumped into her. It was purely hormones and lust.

"I've never been prouder." She wiped away an imaginary tear and beamed with pride. "I won't keep you, but promise me you'll give me all the juicy details tomorrow at lunch."

"Well," I started, threading my fingers through the bag's handle and lifting it from the counter. "When a man and a woman love each other very much . . . "

"I swear I'm going to forget I like you and kick your ass, Sedona." She shoved me good naturedly. "I'm not used to this sassy new you. Who would've thought all you needed was the right guy."

"And the right dick," I blurted, the filter in my brain short-circuiting. It was my turn to gasp out loud at my beyond bold comment. "Damn, I said that out loud."

Callie was all amazement. "I didn't even know you knew that word."

Before I could retort with something sarcastic, a sharp pain exploded in my head, causing me to stumble backward and bang into the counter. The room began to spin, and as Callie's scared features filled my view, I struggled not to throw up.

Something was wrong. This hurt worse than the usual beginnings of a headache or phantom pain.

"Callie," I uttered, groaning through clenched teeth. "Go find him. Tell him." I was now having to breathe through the rapid bursts that had traveled down into my neck. I wouldn't be able to keep upright if this didn't stop.

I missed seeing Callie leave.

Sprawled out on the floor, not caring how it looked, I let out a long groan, and closed my eyes.

The only thought left was this: if this was how I was going to die, at least it was after spending the night with Micah.

Cliché or not, at least I'd be going out with a bang.

CHAPTER 8

$\mathcal{I}$ couldn't keep my eyes off him.

In all fairness, Micah hadn't been able to tear his gaze away either. The dress I'd bought from the consignment store had been worth the investment. I felt absolutely sexy in it. Like I could conquer the world. I couldn't remember the last time I'd worn something that showcased my curves so perfectly.

It was decadent.

Much like the rich, chocolate cake I was eating painstakingly slowly, hoping that it was driving him crazy. For the first time in a long time, I was having an amazing time on our date, and there wasn't anything nagging at me for my attention. I felt brazen sitting beneath the soft glow of mood lighting, the spaghetti strap of my dress having dropped from my shoulder again. This time I didn't bother fixing it.

I wanted Micah to imagine unwrapping me when we got back to my place. Maxwell had agreed to watch Holly another night at her home, so I had my boyfriend all to myself again. I was feeling a little jealous about having to share him, which was strange because that so wasn't who I was.

Yet that feeling swirled about inside my head, messing with my heart. When our waitress had lingered a little longer than I'd liked, batting her eyelashes at Micah, I'd wanted to plunge the spoon deep into her chest. When my fingers slowly wrapped about the silver cutlery, I could see it so clearly in my mind.

The gasp.

The pop that I imagined would happen once my spoon broke through her skin became all I could focus on.

That and the sense of satisfaction.

Instead, I took a large piece of the cake and crammed it in my face. I was a lover, not a fighter.

I would just ignore my wayward thoughts. Perhaps they weren't even mine, and I'd somehow locked onto someone else's emotions, which was terrifying. Who was here that would delight in stabbing someone?

I glanced around nervously, hoping that I'd get some kind of revelation that I wasn't going crazy.

Just crazy in love.

"You're quiet," Micah murmured softly, leaning forward to grab my hand. The mere touch of his fingers sent chills trickling through me. He traced a circle with his thumb, shooting fire down to my toes, all while staring at me, watching for even the smallest of hints.

"I'm just enjoying my dessert," I answered with a smile that I hoped resembled something seductive. "Unless . . ." I was about to be the boldest I'd ever been and pushed away my plate. "You'd rather just go back to my place now and cut to the chase."

He took it in stride. "I've never seen you not finish something sweet."

I locked gazes with him and stretched my foot out underneath the table. I traced the tip of my shoe up his leg until I reached his knee. "There's a first time for everything, right?"

My comment must've confused him, because I didn't get the smile I was hoping for. "Are you sure you're feeling fine? You haven't pushed yourself too much with coming out tonight and planning for the book swap?" He studied me until I squirmed in my seat.

"I've never felt more alive in my life." It was the truth. Sure, I'd just collapsed a few hours ago, but I didn't want to focus on the things I couldn't control. There was no doubt I could conquer the world if I simply set my mind to it, and right now, I was all about conquering the man in front of me.

Hell, forget what I wanted. I *needed* to wrap myself up in him and forget the outside world existed.

Scooping up a dollop of the icing, I savored the taste that flooded my mouth. "Maybe we should get the waitress to box up the entire cake, so we can take it home."

Micah waved to the nearest staff member and made our request. Moments later, the box was at our table, and the check was being paid. He had understood my meaning. I was done with being out and about. I wanted to be home.

Immediately.

The air's chill felt like heaven against my heated skin. It was a beautiful star-filled night in Havenwood Falls, and I craned my neck back to stare up at the sky. Everything was perfect.

"Let's get you home," Micah whispered in my ear after kissing it. He threaded his fingers through mine, and our hands swung between us.

Chocolate and sex. I wondered if Callie had seen that in my future way back at the fair when she'd read my cards.

"You're still quiet." Damn, the man was perceptive. "You'd tell me if anything was wrong, right?" He squeezed my hand. I loved how affectionate Micah could be. Right now, it was driving me insane, because we were still quite a walk from my apartment.

As we passed by the town square, I caught a glimpse of my store. So much had happened in such a short period of time. Taking over the store had made sense back then. It was somewhere safe that I could be free to be myself. I was able to surround myself with the words I loved. I could hide away when reality became too tough and retreat into books.

For a moment there, I'd worried that the incident with Austin had tainted my little niche here in town. I'd been terrified that I wouldn't be able to look past the trauma and reclaim my power. I didn't want to be a victim all my life, and I sure as hell didn't want everyone else viewing me like that either.

Through it all, I'd managed to find a confidence that lit me up from the inside. It was finally my turn to live happily ever after. Tonight was just more evidence that my life truly was magical.

"I promise you I'm fine," I answered, plastering the happiest smile on my face that I could. "In fact, I'm more than fine." A hint of a breeze danced with the hair at the back of my neck. It sent a tickling sensation down through me until it stopped in the pit of my stomach. Then it burst into molten desire.

I tugged on his hand, making him stop. An urgency had taken over as lust drummed a steady beat within my veins. All I could think about was Micah with his mouth all over me, and my mouth—my lips —all over his skin.

"Desperate times call for desperate measures," I mumbled, taking a quick scan of the square for any other pedestrians. It was a quiet night in town. Thankfully, most people were at home, relaxing after a hard day at work. This might work, and I'd be able to cross something off my newly formed bucket list.

Micah stared at me, wearing a quizzical expression. "You're starting to worry me, Sedona."

I placed my finger over his mouth and shushed him. "Trust me. I just had a wicked idea." I slowly started leading him across the street to one of the alleyways that cut between streets. People usually kept to the more well-lit areas in town, and for the most part, the alleyway was reserved for deliveries and dumpsters.

And in this case, a quick pitstop because with each step I took, I felt like I would combust. Something was stirring inside me, and it made me want to scream.

To his credit, Micah didn't argue, and seemed willing to see what crazy plan I was plotting. When we were deep enough in the dimly lit corridor, I whipped about and pushed him hard. I kept pushing him until he backed up against the wall—eyes wide, expectant.

"Sedona." My name on his lips felt like a prayer. He was the only one who'd ever been able to make me react this way from simply speaking my name. It made what I was about to do all the more urgent and necessary.

I took a few steps toward him. "I can't get enough of you, Micah."

His gaze dropped to where I'd placed my hand over his chest.

"There's been something I've wanted to do all evening."

He nodded slightly and licked his lips. I wet mine, too.

"Sedona, I don't think this is the right place for that." He stopped looking at me and peered back to the opening we'd just come from. "Someone might walk past . . . see us. What if the police get a report?"

Sheriff Kasun was a wolf shifter, as were some of his officers. They'd definitely be able to smell the sex in the air.

I didn't care.

"Let them watch."

I waved my hand through the air and uttered a small spell. It was a basic cloaking shield to keep us hidden from prying eyes. It was enough to appease Micah's caution. What I didn't disclose was it didn't prevent those with preternatural senses from knowing something sexual was going on. They could hear.

I silenced Micah with my mouth, my tongue tracing the seam of his lips. Any questions he might have had evaporated into thin air as he snaked his arm around me, anchoring my body to his. The kiss was hot and intense, his fingers digging into my hip. The pain sizzled through my head, and I welcomed it with an outpouring of desire. Every second pushed me closer and closer to losing my mind.

Sex.

It had never been this exciting. It was as though I'd never experienced it before Micah. Perhaps it was his angelic nature, or the fact that I could finally just let go and embrace the moment.

I ground myself against him, feeling him harden beneath my hand as I slid it between us. I couldn't stop myself as I unzipped his pants and freed his erection. The sight of him standing there with his pants to his knees, a hunger blazing from his face, made the risk worth it.

"I came prepared." Lifting the hem of my dress, I revealed a surprise I'd been dying to reveal.

Micah whistled low and long.

I wasn't wearing any panties.

"Sedona." There was so much longing in that one word. "Are you . . ."

I didn't let him finish. With our lips locked and my arms around his neck, I wrapped my legs around his waist. Micah then turned me about so my back was against the cold brick wall.

"Please," I asked.

He answered with a grunt as he slid into me.

We were a perfect fit.

"Don't hold back," I gasped, needing him to throw his protective nature to the side. I wanted to chase this sensation and see where it could take us. Feeling his thickness inside me, I needed him to move. "Now's not the time for gentleness."

I gripped him tightly and rocked forward. Micah's eyes widened, and when I repeated the motion, I witnessed the exact moment he threw caution to the wind as well.

He was magnificent.

As we found the rhythm, the air stilled around us and our muffled cries grew louder. It became easier to forget where we were. The harder and faster he pounded into my body, the more fevered I felt. I relished the soft noise from our bodies hitting each other. It was the most beautiful sound I'd ever heard.

It soon became too much. Titling my head back, I gave in to the magic he was weaving, and held on for dear life. This was transformational. It was epic. It was being etched so deeply into my psyche that I would never forget even the smallest details.

The slickness of his body and mine.

The feel of the bricks against my exposed butt.

The way he leaned into me like I was his salvation.

The way I clung to him like I was drowning.

If this was what addiction felt like—that incessant need and hunger for the one thing that left you feeling alive—then I was addicted to Micah Westbrook.

"Hold on," he warned, before finding some source of energy that had him thrusting harder than before. It was intoxicating. It was exhilarating. It was surreal.

I shattered so hard that there was no catching my breath. I couldn't speak if my life depended on it. All I could do was rest my head forward, completely sheltered by Micah's body. I prayed to God that I wouldn't have to move and place my feet on solid ground again. I didn't want this to end.

"Wow."

It took me a good five minutes to muster the strength to utter it.

"I agree," Micah countered. I loved the wonder that filled his voice. "We can't stay here forever, though. Not like this, at least."

As if to prove his point, a moving shadow caught my eye from my peripheral vision. There was someone paused at the alleyway entrance. "We'll wait for them to leave."

Micah cussed beneath his breath. "You're going to be the death of me," he countered. He slowly lowered me to the ground, careful to make sure I had my balance.

The shadow moved, and whoever it was disappeared from view.

I straightened my dress. "Tell me you don't think this was worth it." I loved teasing him, which was strange, because never in a million years did I think this would be me—completely sexed up in the side street.

Micah grabbed my face and cradled it between his hands. "You will always be worth it." He feathered one more kiss against my lips. "Let me get you home."

Adrenaline coursed through me as we snuck out of the alleyway and continued on our way back to the apartment. The second the door was locked behind us, my dress dropped to the ground. It felt empowering to be naked and carefree.

Micah pulled his shirt off, his eyes never once straying.

He was close enough to catch me when another familiar wave crashed through me.

Pain.

And with that came a scream.

CHAPTER 9

The day had arrived.

Micah and Callie had both tried to tag team me—both equally adamant that no one would be upset if I moved the book swap event back a week. I'd been watched like a hawk after waking up in my apartment, tucked into bed. I'd found a worried boyfriend sitting on a chair he'd dragged in from the kitchen so he could monitor me. When I argued that he could've easily supported me lying beside me under the covers, he'd kindly refuted that it wasn't the time for jokes.

I'd been completely serious. While I had no clue what had taken over my body, I did know how good I would feel with his pressing against mine. He had exactly the right cure for what ailed me. He didn't agree with that, either.

I refused to let their worry sour my excitement. I'd always wanted to do something like this as a way to get the community reading and visiting Shelf Indulgence. In a day and age where books often had to compete with video games, favorite TV show binging, and movie franchises, I needed every advantage I could take.

The imagination was a gift not to be squandered.

As I took care of the last minute details and made sure I had a wide variety of books to choose from, an idea surfaced that actually made me laugh out loud. It would remain a secret that only I knew about, and it would be my gift to the town I loved.

Now the day had arrived, and I was bursting with eagerness. They'd be talking about this small event for years to come. Even the library had offered to donate some of their outdated stock—pairing together with my store to make it a grander affair.

"Sit down for a moment," Micah urged, pushing a glass of water toward me. He was all about keeping me hydrated the past few days. I think that's where we'd kind of landed in diagnosing the pain I'd experienced. While there had been flickers of nausea and dizziness off and on, I'd kept those moments to myself.

It had passed.

Today was a new day, one that I hoped ended with Micah finally seeing that there was no danger, so I could seduce him back into my bed again.

Now that I'd had a taste, I was insatiable.

I tipped the glass backward and drained it. I was tempted to open my mouth and stick out my tongue to prove I'd swallowed it all. There was a layer of annoyance that I couldn't quite shake—I didn't like the attention and people wanting to take care of me.

"Satisfied?" I cocked my brow at him and then returned my focus to the checklist I'd created. Everything was in place. All that was left was officially starting the event. "I gotta go and welcome everyone."

People had started forming groups outside in the town square while they waited. It had warmed my heart to see them holding books, and some had even brought bags filled with them. It was with that confidence that I quickly pecked Micah's cheek and headed toward the door.

My lips were still tingling, my stomach fluttering with nerves.

"Wait, one more for good luck!" Whipping around, I grabbed Micah's face and kissed him hotly. My tongue didn't wait for him to part his lips. It dipped inside, and I moaned, squirming against him. "Okay, maybe two."

My fingers threaded through his hair, curling so I could tug a little. My god, the sensations that coursed through me were intoxicating.

"I'm addicted to you," I murmured against his mouth. "I can't get enough. Is it always like this?" The last part was more for me than him. I didn't really want to hear that he'd had sex like this with someone else. There was a good chance I wouldn't survive the intense jealousy that would follow.

He leaned down until our foreheads touched. His voice was filled with . . . reverence. "I don't think so, Sedona. I think this is just for us."

For us.

Those two words sent my stomach tumbling again, my need to kiss him returning.

A sharp rap at the window broke the moment.

Holly was peering inside, her hands cupped to block out any interfering glare. She pointed to her watch and motioned that it was time.

"Raincheck?" I whispered, grabbing hold of his belt loop.

"Raincheck." He kissed my brow and threw his arms around me for one more hug. "Until then, behave yourself." Micah slapped my butt and led the way to the store's entrance. "And have fun."

"Oh, I plan on it." My gaze shot over to the books I'd wrapped in brown paper and displayed on a large wire shelf.

Then, stepping outside, I welcomed the crowd to Shelf Indulgence.

"Umm, Sedona?" Holly looked like she was terrified as she inched toward me. One of the brown covered books was in her hand, and it looked like it had been hastily rewrapped.

So it begins, I mused. I was surprised it had taken over an hour before someone had brought it to my attention. I wasn't ignorant to the different emotions that swirled about Havenwood Falls. The town had its fair share of scandals and risqué behavior. I also knew that there were some who were a lot more frigid in their views. It was to this group that I'd wanted to cater.

Kind of my way of welcoming them to a world where vanilla was only one flavor in the midst of many.

"What's going on?" I asked, thanking the customer I'd been serving and handing her the bag. We'd had a steady stream of people perusing in and out of the store, and I was ready to call the day a success. My gaze dropped to the package in her hand. "Something wrong?"

"I'll say there's a problem." The screeching voice belonged to Irene Beckett, which was interesting. I'd expected a reaction from one of her cohorts, not her. Irene had always come across as a lady with a colorful past. I'd imagined her huffing and puffing at first, only to drop the book back in her bag before heading home for a night of guilty pleasure reading.

"You didn't find what you wanted?" I looked around them to see if there was anyone else needing my attention. Micah caught my gaze from across the room and mouthed, *you okay?* I waved him off. This wasn't something to worry about.

"What is your excuse for tricking good, upstanding, virtuous members of the community into purchasing such . . ." She sneered at the paper-covered book still in Holly's hands. "Smut." To prove her point, she snatched it out from the young teen's grasp, and held up the cover for all to see. "I heard all about what happens in this story. I'm shocked that you would offer it, Sedona Mathews."

Sixty-Nine by Maddison Grey.

I'd specially ordered them and paid an insanely high price to get them here in time.

The story was one filled with debauchery and erotic pleasure. I'd flicked through the pages last night, which resulted in me using the novel as a fan. The author had spared no description as she told the tale of a young woman coming into her sexuality, exploring the darker, more sensual side of BDSM.

It was the perfect story to open the eyes of the naïve.

It was an intense read that challenged the rigid beliefs some readers held regarding sex and their bodies.

There was no doubt in my mind that Mrs. Beckett hadn't read it yet. She'd taken one look at the sexy cover of a scantily dressed couple in an intimate position and instantly passed judgment. While it wasn't as tame as the covers displayed in the romance section of a chain store, it didn't deserve the tongue-lashing I was having to listen to.

I took the book and brushed my hand over the front. "I still don't see what the issue is. The sign stated clearly that if you were ready for an adventure, the book was for you." I stared back at her. "You agreed to swap."

Her mouth flapped open and closed. Open and closed.

Holly finally chimed in. "Perhaps we can give Mrs. Beckett her book back? Would that make you happy?" She quickly rushed over to the table piled with completed transactions. When she returned, Holly looked to me for approval. "Okay?"

I shrugged my shoulders. "That's up to you, Irene. I quite enjoyed the book, but if you're not ready to take a risk, we'll totally give you your own book back." I all but shoved it at her. "In fact, I insist."

I'd never been so rough with a customer before. I'd had my fair share of difficult people who would take their frustrations out on me, but I'd never crossed that line.

That was, until now.

Micah must've seen me, because one moment, he was across the room, answering questions, and next, he was by my side, his hand firmly at my elbow.

"How about you help Mrs. Beckett find another book, Holly? I need to talk with Sedona about something, and then we'll take care of those." He used his head to point to the discarded title.

He hadn't even finished that when Willow from next door came in, craning her neck until she saw us. She had a brown paper-covered package with the telltale rip showing she'd seen what it was protecting.

"Hey, Sedona, I think there was a mistake made?" She waved the parcel up beside her head.

"I never thought you to be a prude," I blurted out, moments before Micah's hand landed firmly over my mouth.

"Ignore her. Yes, there was a mix up, and we're in the midst of fixing it." He didn't miss a beat, even as I twisted about in his embrace, his other arm snaking around my waist to keep me from breaking free.

Willow eyed me closely. "Is there something I can help with?" She sensed something wasn't right, with her fae abilities that were similar to mine. Despite the chaotic emotions exploding inside me, a small piece of me acknowledged it too.

Did I really just lick Micah's palm?

He didn't flinch.

"Actually, can you help Holly while I figure this out? I just need someone to remove the other wrapped books and make sure no one else has them." He squeezed me hard, hoping it would stop me from squirming. It didn't.

He moved fast, and before I knew it, we were close to the back wall where the door leading up to the apartment was. He didn't go through it, however. Instead, he dropped me back to the ground. His embrace had lifted me up, so it was good to stand on my own again.

"Did you have to?" I asked, straightening my clothes.

"I thought you might need some privacy." The second he realized the way I'd interpreted his comment, he corrected himself. "No, that doesn't mean so we can make out. You're not acting like yourself." This time, when he grabbed the tops of my arms, he wasn't gentle. He stared at me so intently that it made me feel like I was naked.

That thought didn't help matters.

"Why are you always seeing the threat in everything?" My voice rose with frustration. "What's wrong with finally feeling confident?"

"Is that what you call it, Sedona?" Micah pointed over his shoulder in the direction of the entrance. "You purposely antagonized Irene Beckett. You wrapped up an erotic romance book with a misleading invitation. You're not acting like yourself, sweetheart." His tone turned to one that held tenderness. It was easy to see the worry in his eyes.

"I don't know." And that was the truth. I wouldn't deny that things were a little strange, but I still wasn't convinced that the change was unwelcome. I liked the way I'd been feeling. "I really do feel fine."

He was at a loss for words.

I placed my hands against his chest and rose up to kiss his cheek.

"I appreciate your concern, though." When I inhaled, I caught a hint of his cologne. There was no stopping me then as I buried my face in his neck, breathing him in deeply. "Thank you."

I feathered a light kiss against his skin. That kiss led to another. Then another.

"Sedona." There was a firmness in the way he said my name that I didn't like. It was a tone that said he wasn't easily distracted.

"Come on. No one will know." I took hold of his hand and pulled him with me. Each step I took backward brought us closer to escaping upstairs. My fingers were already unbuttoning the top of my jeans.

"Stop!" Micah thundered. His command echoed in my mind. I stopped. All I could do was look up at him with a dumbfounded expression. "This isn't you."

Something inside me snapped. A volcanic heat that began in the tips of my toes and unfurled up through my body until it buzzed loudly against my skin.

"This is me!" I exploded with an anger that was both familiar and foreign. It came from a small place that I pretended didn't exist—a box where I shoved everything I didn't want to share—the dark parts of myself that I refused to acknowledge. "I decide. No one else."

The next part happened so fast that I would later admit there was no possible way I could've stopped.

Stamping my foot in defiance, what I could only describe as an energy wall pulsed out from inside me. The force of the magic blasted over nearby bookshelves. It knocked Micah off his feet, slamming him into the wall that separated Shelf Indulgence from Coffee Haven.

Horror slapped me hard in the face—waking me up from whatever craziness possessed me.

Blood oozed out from the large gash at Micah's temple, but that wasn't what had me screaming.

Somehow, I'd blown a large gaping hole in the wall. Customers who had been enjoying their beverages and pastries were now looking around with confusion. In the midst of heavy dust clouds settling in the air, a flabbergasted Willow appeared.

"I know I joked about you owing me one for helping just now."

She stepped through the newly created doorway into my store. "But this wasn't what I had in mind."

That's when I realized that all eyes were on me. The whispering that was gradually growing louder and louder was about me. No one was interested in the book swap anymore. The show I'd just given everyone was far more entertaining.

"Get me out of here, Micah," I uttered, panic descending.

Something was very, very wrong. The confidence that I'd just been basking in had shriveled into the doubt that now consumed me.

Pain had me doubling over.

I emptied my stomach, the violent retching bringing me to my knees.

Everything went still, and the fear that Micah wouldn't help me became unbearable.

Would he ever be able to trust me again?

"I've got you, sweetheart." His touch sent a wave of calming energy throughout me, and I relaxed into his arms as he picked me up. "I've got you."

That was the last thing I heard as I closed my eyes.

I was safe.

CHAPTER 10

*T*he room was blissfully dark.

Unfortunately, that was the only good thing about being in my grandfather's old bedroom. Micah had chosen to bring me upstairs instead of pushing through the crowd to take me home.

I couldn't really remember much after that. The pain that had taken over everything and stolen my focus was a cruel master. Fiery whips blistered against my skin, making it impossible to do anything but writhe and moan.

Everything hurt.

Existing became intolerable.

The world seemed to press down over me—every thought and feeling screeching to be seen. Nothing made sense. I was suffocating beneath the weight being an empath brought. So much noise. So much suffering.

It blared in my ears and grated over my aura, leaving dark smudges over my psyche. There was no escaping it. Something had broken inside me, and there was suddenly no protective bubble that kept me sheltered from the outside. My own personal warding had been obliterated. It was as if I'd never cast the spells that would help keep me from drowning in the sea of emotions here in town.

A breeze appeared out of nowhere. My body spasmed, and my

back arched up off the bed in agony. My skin was beyond sensitive now. I was slowly losing my mind.

"How can I help?" My heart hurt to hear the depth of helplessness in his hushed question.

I need him to touch me. Only he could soothe the savageness. I balked at the thought. I could barely stand the air caressing my body.

The need was persistent.

"Hold me." The plea was pitiful to the ears, but it was all the strength I could muster.

With painstakingly slow movements, Micah finally relaxed enough beside me, so it didn't feel like I was next to a plank of wood. It took another few seconds before he trusted himself to release his breath.

I stifled the cry that almost escaped when he wrapped his arms about me and pulled me in closer. He knew it had hurt anyway. Where my mouth had obeyed me, the muscles that clenched and trembled had revealed the truth.

"It's okay. It's okay," I repeated, again and again. The mantra matched the one I'd been reciting in my head. Slowly, the pain receded somewhat, enough that I could relax as well.

"Let me heal you."

I let out a tired sigh, wishing I could move so I could look at him properly. I needed him to see how sincere I was. "This is enough, Micah. Just let me lie here with you a little longer." I released the yawn I'd been holding. "Just hold me."

"At least use some of the grace I gave you." This wasn't the first time he'd made this suggestion. It wouldn't be the first time he heard me reply the same.

"No. That's for an emergency, not now. I think all I need is sleep, and I'll be okay. No need to worry." I steeled myself as a short tremor went through me, like the aftershock waves that happen after an earthquake. At least, that's what I told myself.

"Can we talk about what happened downstairs then?"

"No." I shook my head, wincing when my headache flared. "I have no idea how I'm going to face everyone after today. Maybe I should go ask the coven if they could give me a mercy memory wipe or something so I can forget. I'm so mortified."

"I've already taken care of it."

That brought my pity party to an abrupt end. "What do you mean you took care of it?" I asked sharply. "There's a huge freaking hole in the wall of my store, and everyone saw me do it."

"I might be fairly new to town, but I know how these things work. Magic happens, and the coven steps in to cover it up. You might want to thank your aunt for how quickly she got the ball rolling. I might not agree with how she talks to you, but that woman is efficient. The damage is repaired, and memories are being wiped." He gently grazed the side of my face. "The only one who remembers now is you, me, your aunt, and the members of the coven she talked with."

Gratitude crashed through me in waves. He'd stepped in and taken over without me having to ask. This was what it must feel like to be in a relationship with someone who genuinely cared.

He let out a loud groan. "I don't like being this helpless. Not with you. I don't like when unexplained things start happening around those I love."

"You love me?" I asked, teasingly. He'd said it before, but I never tired of hearing it. My lips curled into a soft smile.

Micah chuckled, his chest rumbling beneath my ear. "Focus."

His finger softly brushed across the top of my arm, and the sensation sent goosebumps flaring all over my skin.

As much as I hated being responsible, he was right. Now wasn't the time for distractions. "Raincheck?"

He nodded. "Raincheck."

It was becoming our thing—a way for us to acknowledge something needed to be addressed, but later.

His finger drew a light circle over my bicep.

"Please don't." It had slowly dawned on me that the pain had gradually been fading away. The only thing I could think of being responsible was Micah. "I know what you're doing. You're using your powers when you shouldn't be."

It didn't matter how many times Micah tried to explain he had a little leeway before others would sense his divinity. He argued that it was justifiable, and I countered that unless I was dying, he was never to risk exposing Holly for me that way.

"I'm not, sweetheart." It still thrilled me every time he called me that. "I'm just moving energy about. Trying to see what helps." He hadn't stopped moving his fingers back and forth. Now that I knew, I could definitely feel a pattern emerging.

My moan this time was one of relief. I sunk into the magic his touch was creating, allowing the energy to move about freely. With this new awareness, I could sense how with each stroke of his finger, the more balanced and centered I became. I no longer felt the rawness of pain, or the blistering heat of lust.

I could finally breathe.

"Better?"

My reply was muffled. "Mm-hmm."

"Sedona?"

I was barely awake, sleep tugging at me. "Mm-hmm."

"I protect what I love." There was that word again.

I snuggled into him.

"What happened downstairs wasn't some weird coincidence."

More truth.

I took in a deep breath and then slowly released it.

"I don't think it was, either." I finally admitted what I'd spent days arguing about, desperately trying to convince everyone that all was well. "Something's not right inside me. I can't explain it." That was the thing that sucked. I hated not understanding things.

"I need to find out if this is somehow connected to this Collector person Austin was working for. I know you'd rather just forget everything and move on, but something—or someone—came for Holly, and you got in the way. What if this is some type of payback?"

His response baffled me. "How did you make that leap?"

I watched as his gaze narrowed on me—the way it felt as though he was looking beyond the façade I showed the world and studying something only he could see. I hadn't even considered the person responsible for the attack on Holly and me. Yet, Micah had somehow put two and two together—and came back with five. It made no sense.

I didn't like the way he paused before answering. Only people with something to hide measured each word they said, careful to not reveal too much of their thoughts. I expected this kind of response from Aunt Millicent or those who were merely my acquaintance.

Not the man I loved.

"This isn't going to work between us if we're keeping secrets," I whispered. There was a crack of emotion in my voice—one that hadn't been there before—because all I could think of now was that Micah still didn't trust me enough to confide in me. He'd returned to hiding.

My accusation surprised him. "No, I do trust you, sweetheart. That's not why I mentioned it."

There was no holding back as more doubts filtered through my mind. "Then why did you just hesitate if you weren't trying to censor how you answered my question?" I wasn't going to let this go. "Why do you think the Collector is involved with this? People feel sick all the time, Micah. Maybe I ate something weird, and that's why I feel like this." My hands rested over my stomach as though the mere mention of being ill would bring the symptoms rushing back. "Not everything's an attack."

There was nothing but compassion shining in his eyes now, and he grinned somewhat sheepishly. "Call it an occupational hazard, then. I've been on the run for so long with Holly, always staring into the shadows for hidden danger, that I forget not everyone anticipates threats around every corner."

He took hold of my hand and squeezed it gently. The gesture was meant to be comforting, and it helped a little to settle my rattled nerves.

"I can't imagine what it was like for you to always be looking over your shoulder."

Micah nodded. "You stop seeing the world as your ally, and begin acknowledging that everyone around you holds the potential to become your enemy. I've kept Holly safe so far because I no longer consider the inconsequential or smaller reasons behind things."

It was starting to make more sense. "So you just instantly go for the worst case scenario."

His smile lit up his face. "Exactly. Chances are that ninety-nine point nine percent of what's happening to you right now can be resolved with a simple explanation. I *have* to entertain that point one percent, however."

"And that's the Collector?" Just mentioning the name of the mystery threat made my skin crawl. I tried to ignore the fact they were still out there somewhere—possibly watching. "So this could be a second attack?" It still felt weird to make that assumption.

He nodded again. "Possibly."

An even more horrifying thought surfaced.

"What if it is, then?" Now that we were talking about him, the thought sat like a heavy rock of dread in my gut. The very notion that I was a pawn in this mysterious being's game sickened me.

Tears began to fall.

"I'm going to demand a meeting with the Court again tomorrow, and I won't leave until they answer my questions. Every. Single. One."

"And if they don't give them to you?"

"Let me worry about that. Close your eyes again and try to sleep some more." I could feel him moving my energy around again, his touch now filled with magic.

"We'll figure it out," I murmured.

Hope filled my heart, but not before a sliver of fear wormed its way in.

The Collector.

Was I losing my mind or was there really someone out there seeking retribution against me?

Like always, the answer danced out of my reach—taunting me.

In my dreams, it haunted me.

CHAPTER 11

$\mathcal{S}$helf Indulgence remained closed the next day.

As far as I was concerned, I never wanted to step foot outside the upstairs apartment. Even with Micah trying to convince me that it wasn't as bad as I imagined, I was content to ignore the world outside.

Thoughts about my outburst piled up inside my head until I wanted to scream for the noise to stop.

Micah had remained by my side, only taking breaks to ensure Holly was still okay out in the living room. She'd come upstairs once the crowd had dissipated, locking up the store while the Court took care of magically fixing the damage I'd caused. No one had asked her to. Instead, she saw a need and filled it.

Micah had just finished the last energy treatment in balancing out the power that came and flared like the tides submitted to the moon. I was already beginning to feel edgy—the benefits of his touch fading away faster today. The pain that remained was manageable.

The lust . . . it was torture to have him so close and not be consumed by him.

There was a tiny tap at the door to warn me I was about to have a visitor. I'd refused everyone so far, and I didn't hide my surprise when

Holly popped her head through the crack in the door. "Someone wants to talk to you." She seemed twitchy—antsy.

Before I could question her, my aunt pushed her way past, dismissing Holly with the order to close the door.

"What are you doing here?" I asked. She was the last person I wanted to see right now. Her very presence grated against my skin, creating a new wave of pain. She'd broken my heart with her refusal to see me as anything other than someone to manipulate.

"What's happened to you is no excuse for such rudeness. If you can't speak to me with respect as your family, then you will show me it because of my position within the coven." There wasn't a hint of compassion in her words. Once again, she'd waltzed in and with all the condescension she could muster, made herself the victim.

I was the one being rude.

I was the one causing her distress.

If I had the strength, I would've stood up and tossed her out of my home on her ass. Rage sprung to life as I remembered every disagreement we'd ever had. All the cruel words she'd said for my "benefit."

She was spared from any confrontation by Micah's return. The moment he saw her standing there in front of me, he rushed in and made her step back. He wanted her nowhere near me.

"I don't think this is the time, Ms. Mathews," he began, forcing her toward the door by taking a step toward her. He could be extremely menacing when he chose to be.

"While I can admire your willingness to protect my niece, I'm not here on personal matters. I come on behalf of Saundra Beaumont. She felt, considering our familial relationship, it would be better if I come and investigate the magical mishap from yesterday. I thanked her for her generosity." Millicent watched me like she expected me to agree or profess my love and loyalty to the witch. I hated seeing the know-it-all shine in my aunt's eyes. She was itching to say it.

I could feel it.

"If you could kindly invite Saundra to meet with me, I'll gladly answer any questions she might have." It was Micah who answered.

"In fact, I'll be willing to sit down and have a conversation with anyone who might answer my questions."

"This doesn't concern you, Mr. Westbrook. I thank you for taking care of Sedona, but this is a family matter now. You're welcome to come back in once I've finished my discussion with my niece." She had the audacity to look down her nose at him.

Micah took one more step toward her. "Everything that concerns Sedona concerns me. So I repeat, please arrange a meeting between Saundra and myself. I understand you're just doing your job." He said the last few words as though he mocked them. "But I don't believe in passing notes back and forth with a messenger."

She actually spluttered, spittle flying from her mouth. "Watch your tone, Mr. Westbrook. I am not someone you'd want to make an enemy of."

He didn't budge. Instead, Micah inclined his head in acknowledgment. "I would give you the same warning. I am older than you think. I have wielded power beyond your comprehension."

Aunt Millicent didn't shrink away. If anything, she grew taller, standing her ground. "Is that a threat?" Whenever she got excited, her voice rose a few octaves, sounding higher pitched than usual.

Like right now.

Dogs could've heard her from miles away.

She was used to intimidating people and had finally met her match with Micah. He didn't cower when she pulled out her phone and started dialing a number. No matter how hard she glared at him, Micah didn't falter.

It was beautiful to watch.

"He's requesting an audience with you." The person on the other end answered quickly. "I explained that." She nodded. "Okay. Thank you."

The conversation lasted thirty seconds max.

"Ms. Beaumont asks that you answer the questions I have, and once she's read my report, she'll arrange a meeting. Not a second before."

Something told me that her response had everything to do with her annoyance at Micah trying to summon her, and less because she didn't have time. People very rarely talked to the high priestess of our coven that way.

He turned to look at me. "Are you up to this?"

Peering around him to my aunt, I wanted to tell him no. I would never be okay talking with this woman who was hell-bent on always misunderstanding me.

But this was town business—at least the large hole was. The sooner we had this conversation, the sooner she could leave.

I nodded. "Just don't leave me here alone with her." I guided his hand to my thigh as he came to sit by me on the bed. If he could help me manage my outbursts by moving about the energy, then I'd be okay.

I wouldn't suddenly act on my need to blast away my aunt.

There was that anger again.

"Micah," I croaked. The flares were happening more often now.

Aunt Millicent completely ignored the brief interaction. "We need to talk about what happened yesterday, Sedona." Before I could interrupt her, she waved her hand dismissively. "And no need to thank me. It's what family does . . . we step in and clean up messes."

Oh, she was especially snippy today.

All I could do was hope my honesty would soften her demeanor. "I honestly don't know. I've been feeling off for the past few days. I remember that I was angry, and then Micah refused." I glanced sideways to where he was listening. Thankfully my aunt didn't ask me to elaborate on what his refusal meant. "And the next thing I know, everything goes flying and boom! A hole."

If she pursed her mouth any harder, her lips would've snapped off completely. "People don't just expel that level of power and magic by accident without some kind of reason. Have you been tinkering about up here in your grandfather's study?" There was a flash of pride in her eyes. "Did you finally take my advice and start honing your skills?"

That reason seemed to please her the most. It was almost cruel to shatter her newly found hope that yesterday was simply a case of a spell gone awry.

"No." I didn't mince words. "And that's exactly what I'm saying. It was an accident."

Micah coughed.

"I suppose you have something to add." I was embarrassed by how patronizing she sounded talking to Micah. Her position within the coven had made her arrogant. She was talking to someone who held more power in his pinky finger than she did in her whole body. She'd either completely drank the special brand of Kool-Aid—loyal to a fault to Roman Bishop and his fellow cronies—or she had no sense of self preservation.

Micah let her superiority complex slide off him like water off a duck's back. "I believe she's being attacked, or at the very least, targeted."

She openly mocked his statement. "By whom? Who would be interested in Sedona? She's a young girl who runs a bookstore. She has nothing to offer. What potential she has, she squanders."

This time I did wince. "I'm sitting right here. I can hear you, Aunt Millicent."

She brushed me off with a wave of her hand. "I'm done mincing words with you. I've done all I can to help you, and you reject each of my suggestions and attempts. I ask for honesty from you and return it to you in kind. So again, I ask what happened yesterday. I need something to report."

Micah began to stand and defend me, but I couldn't bear for him to break contact with my skin. He was what was tethering me to the sane part of my psyche. If he stopped, I wasn't sure I could hold my temper back.

"I already told you. I've been feeling weird the past few days. At first, I didn't think much of it. I was actually enjoying feeling stronger." That wasn't the word I meant. "No, it was more than that. I felt confident."

Her face went white as the blood drained out of her cheeks.

"Confident?" There was a slight hitch in her voice.

"But it was more like confidence on crack." That description would have to do. "It just kept building and building until it had nowhere else to go but out." I made an explosion gesture with my hands. "There were other side effects that came along with the new feeling." My cheeks were already starting to flush. "Didn't really have a problem with it."

I winked at Micah. The smile he gave me in return lifted part of the weight that I felt pushing down on me.

"Describe these side effects." She was poised to write them down in the notebook she'd pulled out from her bag.

I didn't answer.

She repeated the question. When I kept quiet, she turned to Micah. "What am I missing here?"

Confusion blazed across her face.

"Sex," I blurted. "One of the side effects was sex. Lots and lots of amazing sex. Do you still want details?" I threw the challenge down at her feet. I didn't have the patience to side step her attitude.

Millicent stopped writing. "That wasn't necessary either, Sedona."

There was one word written on the page, and with an angry scribble, she wrote over it. Then she grew quiet—too quiet.

"What are you thinking?" It was Micah who asked. He moved his hands, and I loved the way the heat from his touch followed.

I wished we were alone, so I could have him touch me all over.

I wanted to touch him.

My breath caught, and I whipped out to grip his hand tightly. I couldn't have these feelings right now—not when I couldn't trust myself to control them long enough not to put on a show for Millicent.

"Just breathe through it," he whispered softly in my ear. "Don't forget I've got you."

"I believe I know what caused this." Her words brought everything crashing to a halt. Even Micah stared at her with disbelief. "And before I explain, please know I did it with the purest of intentions."

A sickly feeling filled my stomach.

I didn't want to hear whatever she was ready to confess. It couldn't be anything good.

"I'm listening." There was a steely menace in the undercurrent of Micah's response.

I closed my eyes. If I couldn't see her speaking, in my tired brain, that meant it wouldn't hurt more. God, I needed this all to stop hurting.

"I cast a spell."

The room felt like even it took a gasp of shock.

"Excuse me?" I asked, just to make sure I'd heard her correctly. "You cast a spell on whom?"

Please don't say it. Please don't say it.

I'd read somewhere that one of the best ways to deal with hearing bad news was to not avoid its existence, but to repeat your exposure to it. At the time it had made sense, but that was the opposite of what I was thinking right now.

I didn't want the truth to come out.

I didn't want to hear the dangerous lengths my aunt would go to just to prove she was right.

She'd cast some powerful magic.

She'd enchanted me.

"Whom?" Micah pushed, no longer trying to hide the anger he was feeling.

"After our last argument, I went home and cast a confidence spell on your behalf." She made sure to rush out that last piece of justification quickly, as though it would somehow redeem her shitty actions. "It was with the best intentions. I wanted to show you that I'd heard you when you said you weren't as confident as everyone else when it came to your powers. I knew you wouldn't try to find a cure for those doubts, so I wanted to help you along."

"So you turned me into a raging nympho?" Everything about this conversation was surreal.

"No," she exclaimed equally fast. "I meant no harm."

"Then explain the hole in the wall." Micah sat calmly beside me. I wondered if that was also for my benefit, because he was still trying to manage my own imbalance. "Explain why she can barely tolerate other people unless I'm right there beside her . . . grounding her."

Aunt Millicent's gaze dropped to where his hands were. "It wasn't meant to do that." She shook her head, confused. "I was very specific that my spell and magic helped Sedona face and conquer her greatest fear."

"And you assumed that was my powers?" It was slowly starting to make sense.

"Isn't it?"

She *still* didn't get it. I wasn't afraid of my powers, because I didn't plan on using them. I was content to be empathic and leave the rest for anyone else who was interested. The town wasn't short on magic. There would be plenty of others who would fill the void I made by not embracing the full extent of my magic.

"No. My greatest fear at the moment is being with Micah and taking the next step in our relationship." I turned to face him. "I've been worried about ruining what we have with each other by rushing things. I worried that I wouldn't measure up—that somehow I would disappoint." I shrugged my shoulders with the hope that it hid my embarrassment. It was hard enough telling this to Micah, without my aunt listening in as well.

He gently kissed the back of my hand. "You think too much."

His smile was my reward for being brave and sharing how I felt. I didn't pretend that every thought and feeling I had was completely rational.

"Oh." That's all she would say.

Micah didn't have such problems. "Remove the spell now. Whatever you did, reverse it."

This time, Aunt Millicent didn't resist his demands or reply with some snotty remark meant to put him in his place.

"I'm going to need a candle."

When he returned with a small white pillar, Millicent had finished scribbling something on a piece of paper.

"She's going to need a lighter or matches so she can use the candle's flame to burn her spell." I knew which one she'd used and how to counteract it. Millicent had tweaked it enough, so she was the only one with authority to break it. So simple.

The air stilled. No one said a word. When she was finally ready, she began uttering out loud, her voice gradually growing stronger and stronger. The flame danced about as if it eagerly awaited its chance to burn. It wasn't until the last fragment of paper crumpled into ash that I felt another shot of pain.

Scratch that. An avalanche of agony that never relented, never subsided. Instead of making everything better and ending this nightmare, whatever spell she'd cast had backfired horribly.

"Micah!" I screamed, as the energy inside me reached a dangerously fevered pitch.

"Get down!" he yelled in return, throwing his body over mine.

Time stood still.

The energy reached its crescendo.

It became all I could feel, see, hear, and smell.

I became it.

And then everything fell apart.

CHAPTER 12

"Something struck back!" I couldn't quite catch my breath with my lungs burning for air. There was no escaping the pain as I frantically clawed at my throat. It felt like someone was shredding my insides Freddy Krueger–style.

"Tell me what's happening." It was Aunt Millicent who filled my vision.

"You're trying to kill me!" My voice was raw and guttural. It took everything in my diminishing power not to hurl all over her. "You fried my circuits and broke me!"

"Always so dramatic," she complained, as she hovered her hands over my body. Electricity crackled between us, but nothing she did seemed to help. If anything, it made things worse. Like a bear woken from hibernation too soon, whatever magic coursed through my veins had created a monster—one that roared in fury for being disturbed.

"Get out." I was done. Grabbing Micah, I begged him to kick her out. She had caused this, and if she didn't quit judging me, I was going to unleash my temper at her. It was white hot and ready to scorch the world.

"You need me." She hadn't even budged, ignoring my demand. "You've neglected your powers, so you're useless to help." She just kept talking, oblivious to the way it felt like daggers in my heart. Her words wielded more damage than the chaos whipping my psyche into a frenzy.

"You're wrong," Micah barked. He wore a grim expression as he cradled me in his arms, hoping that the more he touched me, the more he could soothe the pain. I saw him tug at the leather cord around his neck. It was a Celtic carving that was shaped into a sigil. He hadn't taken it off in all the time I'd known him, and the energetic juice that radiated from the piece told me that it was used in hiding his divine nature.

The strap snapped, and I gasped in horror.

"No!" I exclaimed, surging forward to refasten it around his neck. "Don't you dare, Micah. Don't you dare take that risk."

His hand burned bright as a yellow glow started emanating from his palm. "I won't lose you. Not like this." And without any warning, he pressed his hand firmly over my forehead, his fingers gripping my temples. "I'm sorry, Sedona."

Then he blasted me with a shot of angel grace—his healing touch sweeping into my body, purifying me as it flowed. All the while I murmured how much I needed him to stop. He couldn't jeopardize Holly's safety by putting my needs above hers. It wasn't about being a martyr or wanting to die.

I just couldn't stand the idea of something happening to my sweet young friend.

The fear of the consequences should the worst truly happen felt overwhelming. Micah would never forgive himself. I would never forgive myself for my role in it. It would sit between us—the large, angry, painful wound that would destroy whatever relationship remained.

I couldn't live with that.

With what little strength remained, I pried Micah's fingers back and shoved him away. At least that was what I'd planned on doing if something else hadn't moved him for me.

He yelled in surprise as he slammed backward, a few feet away.

"Micah?" Aunt Millicent called out to him and wore the same grim expression he did. "What happened?"

There was a muffled groan from his direction.

My aunt doubled her efforts in trying to end my suffering.

I began to writhe. Without Micah's help, I was left open and vulnerable to the continued attack.

And then, just like that, it was over. If it hadn't been for the way my muscles throbbed and ached, the pulsing tempo in my head, and the slick coating of sweat over my skin, I'd have thought I'd imagined the past ten minutes.

Micah came to with a start. I didn't know who was more confused —him for waking up and being across the room, or me and the new wave of blissful relief that took over my body.

"You okay?" I croaked, desperately trying to wet my lips.

"Yes, you?" It didn't take him long to return back to his normal self. When he gingerly went to lift me so he could hold me, I stunned him further.

"I don't hurt anymore," I whispered. There was a niggly fear that if I said that any louder, it would jinx whatever blessing I was enjoying. I was scared that the mayhem would return.

My aunt studied me closely, pushing her glasses back toward her face. There was no mistaking her look of skepticism. Unlike her, however, I didn't want to look the gift horse in the mouth.

"We should still try to figure out what happened, Sedona," she said, staring down at her hands. "I can't take credit for your respite. We can't guarantee that the pain won't return."

I closed my eyes in denial, hoping I could ignore her logic. I was tired—exhausted from the relentless battering I'd just withstood. I was emotional from being so raw. All I wanted to do was go home and climb into bed with my boyfriend and forget this ever happened.

"I agree." That was the last thing I'd expected Micah to say. Apparently, Aunt Millicent felt the same. "Don't look at me like that. I'm only saying that I'm not comfortable with celebrating just yet. We still need answers."

His explanation was meant to keep her from acting pious and smug.

"I will need to inform the coven. We should be able to uncover the cause with their aid." Once again, her response was to take over and place her faith in those who watched over Havenwood Falls.

I didn't have that kind of loyalty. "No, I don't want to involve them."

She scolded me. Like honest to goodness, shook her finger at me. "It's not up to you, Sedona. They're better equipped to handle something like this."

I tuned her out and turned to Micah instead. "Take me into my grandfather's study."

An idea had floated its way to the surface of my mind. Like the inspiration had been heaven sent from him, a memory tickled at my senses.

Micah didn't argue with me, something I was incredibly grateful for. As he gathered me up in his arms, not letting me stand on my own, I motioned for him to stop for a moment. "Here's the deal, Millicent. You can either come with me into the study and do our best to figure out what the hell you did so we can fix it—"

"Or?" There was a touch of defiance in the way she held my gaze.

"Or you can leave. Not to bring the coven back here. Simply leave. If you choose not to be part of the solution, you become part of the problem. I'm done fighting with you. I don't have the energy anymore to battle with you over the dumbest things. So decide." I nodded to Micah. "Let's go."

I didn't wait to see if she'd get up and follow. In my heart of hearts, I'd already dismissed her because my aunt was nothing if not consistent. Her loyalty to me as her niece would be once again pushed to the side. The truth that always lay between us was that she felt more loyalty to her own deluded sense of importance than me.

For as long as I could remember, she'd used her connections with the Court and coven to badger and belittle me over my life choices. Whenever I chose not to follow in my aunt's footsteps and show her the exaggerated respect she believed she deserved, it had been one judgmental comment after another.

I was never good enough.

I would always be a failure in her eyes—ignoring my supposed family legacy within the coven by neglecting my gifts.

I was only now ready to accept the fact that there would be no pleasing her—ever.

Once inside the study, the enormity of what had just occurred sent convulsions through me. Hot tears streaked down and over my cheeks. Sorrow and grief burst outward in the form of loud sobs. After trying so hard to keep it together and prove to myself—to others—that I could overcome whatever life threw my way, there was no more pretending.

I didn't hold it back or push it down so I could ignore it.

I cried for myself.

I cried for my grandfather who had left a hole in my heart when he died.

I cried for Micah and Holly—the life they'd been forced to live in order to survive.

I cried for Austin, who had been banished from town already, his memories stripped.

And I cried for my aunt, the one person who couldn't figure out that true power, lasting power, was found in the bonds you created with others. Family. Friends. Not merely connections with those who held the coveted influence and authority.

Micah continued to hold me, rocking me gently as his hand rubbed my lower back.

In the quiet minutes that followed, his tender touch was enough.

THE TIME HAD COME.

I could already feel the heated sensation building inside me again. Aunt Millicent's spell had been removed for a solid hour, and we'd hoped that with it, all the craziness would be gone. But something had pushed back. Another spell. Something.

My body screamed in protest as I moved, my muscles wanting to hold on to the peaceful respite Micah's arms had provided. He hadn't left my side the whole time. I hated knowing that he was worried, because he already had so much to focus on. The sooner things went back to normal, the better.

"Rest some more." Micah's deep voice filled the study.

He reluctantly released me from his embrace, and I slowly stood up and stretched.

"It's stirring again, so I need to find out what it is now." Helping him stand, I let out a lengthy breath. I knew the ritual needed. The inspiration had come earlier while I was resting, and it would be a doozy. I didn't even know if I held enough magic to perform it. It was usually a spell that called for two or more witches.

"Okay, how can I help, then?" He left my side to go look at one of the six bookshelves that filled the room. It wasn't just the love of Shelf Indulgence that I inherited from my grandfather. I'd also shared his deep passion for the written word. He'd spent his life accumulating these powerful tomes filled with our family's history, and kept the family's book of shadows. That was the volume I looked for now.

"There's nothing much you can do," I admitted, flipping through the book Micah had handed me until I found the incantation. A few summers ago, my grandfather and I had been talking about some of his experiences growing up. He'd mentioned a spell he'd been part of that helped the coven find out the truth in a bitter argument between two coven members. It was this spell that I was now trying to read and understand. "Usually this is done with more than one witch. One person says the words and uses the others to help channel as much power as possible."

We were at a disadvantage, and he knew it. "Will having an angel with you help?"

It was the question I'd dreaded. "If you weren't currently hiding from some big bad and protecting an adorable teenager, I'd totally suggest we give it a try." I winked at him with the hopes it softened my sarcasm. "Thanks for the offer, though."

"Then tell me what will happen if you don't have enough juice to fuel this spell."

My mouth went dry. I didn't want to answer him with the truth, because then he would fight for me to abandon the plan.

"She doesn't need to worry about that. She has me."

Speak of the Devil, and she comes.

"I was serious before," I countered, not wanting her involvement if it meant she couldn't let go of her unrealistic expectations. "I don't need or want your help if it comes with conditions."

Aunt Millicent lifted her hands in surrender. "You can't do that spell alone. It'll kill you."

Micah's nostrils flared in surprise. "Sedona? Is she right?"

I felt the pressure to answer like a ten-ton weight pressing against my chest. "Well . . ." He wasn't impressed at all by my nonchalant shrug.

"No," Micah thundered, flashing me a glare filled with the power he held as an angel. "Absolutely not. I'm not going to let you risk yourself that way."

"You're not going to let me?" I threw back, just as forceful. "Last time I checked, Micah Westbrook, I didn't need your permission for anything." I stood with my hands on my hips, glowering.

"You know that's not what I meant, sweetheart." Gone was his anger. "You told me we were in this together, so let's stick with that plan. There has to be something else."

Aunt Millicent had remained uncharacteristically quiet up until now. As she turned through the pages of our family's book of shadows, I could sense a longing I'd never felt from her before. I would almost call it homesickness. Before I could see where the emotional tether would lead, she spoke up.

"I'll ensure she's protected, Mr. Westbrook." She turned to me with a look of determination. "I'll get the supplies needed. You need to ground yourself before you start." Then she walked about in search of the candles, crystals, and herbs needed.

Micah watched her go and then grabbed me by the arm. "Explain it to me. The ritual. Tell me what it involves." He didn't trust my aunt either.

"It's simple enough," I started, hoping to minimize his concern. "It requires me to untether myself from this reality and in spirit form, conjure up what I'm asking to see. I want to see why I've been feeling so strange and whether it's a byproduct of my aunt's interference."

I heard her grunt quietly. I still didn't know how I felt about her using her magic against me.

"And why do you need others to help, if it's that simple?"

"Because magic always comes with a price, and if I'm found unworthy, then my abilities might not be enough to bring me back." I grabbed his hands and squeezed them reassuringly. "I don't know any other way that can give me the answers I need so quickly."

Aunt Millicent chimed in. "Go before the coven and ask for their help." She'd placed the last of the white candle pillars at a point in the pentagram that was permanently etched into the study's wooden floor. "Put aside your pride and insecurities, Sedona. I can even come with you if need."

Micah went still as he thought. "I don't trust you." His sole focus was now on my aunt. "If you use this in any way to hurt her, I will destroy you."

She had the common sense to look shocked by his blatant threat. "You don't scare me, Mr. Westbrook."

"I don't care. Are we understood?" Micah would never back down. He looked every inch the avenging angel right now as he stared her down. "You protect her like the aunt you *should* be and we won't have an issue."

There was a tiny nod from her. "You have my word."

My chest was starting to hurt, and it made me audibly gasp. If I didn't get to chanting, the next wave of pain would hit. I was done feeling like crap.

"Stop. I'm ready to begin. Micah—" I gave him a quick hug, kissing his cheek. "I need you to guard the door just in case someone decides to interrupt." I waved my hand through the air, and the flames from all the candles in the room burst to life. "Aunt Millicent, I need you to join me in the pentagram."

We both sat inside, our legs crossed, and I held my hands out for her to hold. I stared hard into her eyes, drawing on my empathic gifts to see if there was any kind of ulterior motive behind her willingness to help.

Nothing. She was being honest. Knowing this made it a little easier to relax.

"You know what to do, right?" I asked, needing to make sure we were both on the same page. A lot could go horribly wrong with this spell. "Don't break the connection between us once I start. You're going to feel that sharp tug on your magic. Don't resist it."

She actually snorted at me. "I know the incantation, Sedona. I've been doing circle magic and rituals long enough, I could perform them flawlessly in my sleep." When she realized how snarky her reply sounded, she smiled to soften it. "Sorry, old habits die hard." Gripping my hands tighter, Aunt Millicent nodded. "I'm ready."

Words began to spill from my lips. Summoning the elements to bless the spell came next, and I took comfort as I felt each one present itself to my circle. I called on my ancestors, my grandfather in particular, to give aid to my request. When I felt the familiar energy of my mother, tears formed in my eyes.

It was now or never.

Electricity sparked in the air above us and like a portal from another world, a glowing oval appeared above me. The more I chanted, the bigger it became, until it resembled the television screen I had back home. It kept growing the more power I fed the spell.

"It's working," I whispered, so the others would know. "All that's left is to ask."

The two-verse incantation lay before me as I quickly read from the page. When I finished, a mighty blast passed through the room, and for a tiny second, I was worried my aunt would let go of my hands.

"I've got you," she countered through clenched teeth. Sweat formed at her brow before trickling down the side of her face. Strain filled her features. The price was already being exacted for my request.

My own body was under attack as the pain came rushing back. What started as a whimper became an unbearable moan, my body trembling to maintain control of the magic.

"Sedona," Micah called out, checking to see if I was okay. Before he could take a step toward me, I told him to stop. It was too late to go back now.

"Show me," I asked, tilting my head back to the ceiling. "Show me the cause for the pain that racks my body."

Time slowed down, and a hush descended upon us. At first, I couldn't make anything out from the vision that was forming within the cloud above me, but then it became crystal clear.

I instantly recognized the scene of me and Micah walking along the street together. I remembered the moment, the discussion we'd been having. It wasn't until something caught my eye after bumping into someone that I grew excited.

"There. Did you see that?" Without letting go, I leaned closer to my aunt. "That person. It's not a spell."

"No, it isn't," she whispered back, stunned.

"Is that . . . ?" Even Micah was dumbfounded.

It hadn't been my aunt's spell backfiring.

The stranger I'd passed in the street was responsible for the hell and agony I'd been through.

That, and the magical marking they placed on me.

I'd been tagged with something powerful.

I was in deep trouble if I didn't figure out how to remove it.

Immediately.

CHAPTER 13

"*G*et it off her," Micah demanded, his anger aimed toward my aunt. Even though the spell had revealed the person had transferred their own branding spell separately from her interference, he was holding her responsible for the attack.

If looks could kill, she'd be six feet under already.

"While I appreciate your anger," she fired back, her eyes never straying from me, "I need to concentrate on helping my niece." Hearing her support tugged at my conscience. Perhaps our relationship could be redeemed. "Focus, Sedona. How are you feeling?"

I tested my energy reserves and nodded. "I'm good. Why?" I was out of my depth now.

"Because I'm going to help you get rid of the mark without it killing you."

It was a night of constant shocks. My by-the-book, rule-loving aunt was suggesting we bypass seeking the counsel of her beloved coven. It was enough to make me look at her differently.

She'd begun turning me about, looking for the physical evidence that I'd been tagged. "You're going to need to take your shirt off. It'll be small . . . perhaps something you'd glance over or not even see." Her fingers roamed roughly over my skin—not because she wanted to hurt me, but because time was of the essence. "Help me, Micah."

The shocks kept coming.

"I don't know what to do," I confessed, bracing myself for the lecture that usually followed after such admissions.

There was none. "I do, Sedona. It's going to be extremely tricky, but we can do this together." She smiled at me. An honest-to-goodness genuine smile. That was a miracle in and of itself.

"This," Micah finally exclaimed, and they both went quiet as they leaned in. I could feel their warm breaths over the bottom of my left shoulder blade, tickling a little. "At first I thought it was a large freckle, but it kind of zapped me when I brushed my finger over it."

Aunt Millicent released a soft mm-hmm. She gingerly scraped at it with her fingernail. "This might hurt, Sedona."

With her palm placed firmly over the would-be freckle, I heard her whisper a short incantation seconds before an excruciating wave of pain blasted through me.

I dropped to my knees. I couldn't keep standing, even if I wanted to. Crackling energy blistered beneath the spot, and I could feel it sizzling the nearby nerve endings.

"What. The. Hell?" My question came out through clenched teeth. There was no end to the pain—no light at the end of a very dark tunnel. My fingers clawed at the wooden flooring until finally the intensity lessened. "If that's what happens just from touching the damn thing, how am I going to survive removing it?"

I hated how weak I sounded . . . how small my voice was.

Aunt Millicent was uncharacteristically quiet until she finally broke the silence. "I've never experienced this strength of magic before."

Her confession terrified me.

"Never?" I croaked, my throat dry.

"It's very old." There was an undeniable fear in her tone that overshadowed the reverence she usually felt for power and magic. I almost wanted to ask her more questions, but then some hidden switch inside her flipped, and she was back to being the arrogant witch I knew. "But that won't stop me from removing it."

She touched the mark one more time, the gesture almost like a caress.

"What do you need?" Micah interrupted. "I can get it for you."

My aunt looked about at the items that surrounded us. "I need something sharp to cut with." Then, as if to clarify, she corrected herself. "An athame. It has to be imbued with power for it to work."

That made my heart race quickly.

"Do I want to know?" I asked skeptically.

"There's always a price when it comes to power and using your gifts. Sometimes it's small, but in a case like this, a great sacrifice is needed."

Blood. She meant blood would need to be spilled to fuel the spell. Blood magic was something I'd never practiced. In fact, everything about that branch terrified me. I'd rather willingly watch every scary horror movie ever produced . . . nonstop . . . in the dark . . . alone . . . than perform anything remotely connected to it.

Micah returned from the table that held my grandfather's tools. Handing my aunt the athame our family's patriarch used most, he lingered close just in case. We were still somewhat leery of her newfound sense of family and loyalty.

Twice bitten, twice shy.

"I'm going to cut my palm and then yours, Sedona." She let go of one of my hands, careful not to let go of the other. "Just for a moment. When I've completed the task, we'll hold hands again, and I'll recite the incantation, then remove the mark from your body. The magic won't like that we're interfering with the spell's intention, but this is the only way. You ready?"

Time was going so quickly that I didn't have a moment to pause and argue. The pain was growing stronger and stronger, making it hard not to wince with each beat of my heart. The spirit inside was angry it'd been discovered.

"Yes." I bit my bottom lip as she sliced across my palm.

"Now me." She repeated the motion. Then she squeezed my fingers, and in a tone I rarely heard, she said, "I love you, Sedona. I'm sorry I wasn't the aunt I should've been. I was wrong to push you so hard. I just hope that this will make up for my foolish pride."

Her words stoked up fear. They sounded more like a goodbye than an apology.

"What do you mean?" I asked, feeling edgier by the second. I glanced over at Micah, who was staring at my aunt like he'd never seen her before.

That's when it dawned on me.

She *was* saying goodbye.

As the words for the spell left her lips, I heard the truth—she was taking my place—welcoming the spirit to leave my body and enter hers.

"No!" I screamed, trying to let go of her so the connection would break. I didn't care if the magic bounced back and hit me with all its might. I wasn't even thinking that my reaction might kill me. All I could see was the peaceful face of my aunt as she accepted responsibility.

She clung to my hands, refusing to drop them.

I struggled to slip from her grasp and failed.

All the while, I watched in horror as I felt a malevolent energy push against my skin and then burst out of my body. A black form appeared beside us in the pentagram. At least, that's what it looked like to me. Whatever it was, it wouldn't be able to go far. It was trapped in here as long as the circle held true.

"Micah, go get Saundra." She was in over her head and would need the high priestess to come help. "Find her and explain what happened. Tell her to come quickly."

Indecision warred in his eyes. "I don't want to leave you."

I loved him for that.

"Trust. Isn't that the foundation of a successful relationship?" I threw him the best smile I could muster.

"Doesn't mean I like any of this." His weary smile helped soothe my own exhaustion. I felt beat up.

"We're going to be okay. Promise." I looked nervously at my aunt, who had closed her eyes. I didn't like how quiet she was. "Now go. Please."

A deep, guttural sound erupted from my aunt's mouth. "No. Wait."

Her eyes flew open, and she stared vacantly, as though she was blind. I'd never seen her look like this before, and her voice . . . it wasn't her own.

It belonged to the one responsible for this very ugly and nasty piece of magic.

"My work is done here. Consider this another warning. Get in the way again, and everyone you love will die."

The message was directed to Micah as Aunt Millicent's mouth moved effortlessly—her eyes blank.

"What are you?" I asked, needing to know who was threatening us. I grabbed my aunt tightly, tempted to shake her hard so the spirit would answer. "Who are you?"

My blood ran cold as I became its focus. "I am but a messenger. They are coming."

Before either of us could speak, my aunt began to convulse. She was fighting against the spirit—and from the looks of it, she was losing.

"Micah, I need you!" I cried out. I was desperately trying to channel every ounce of energy I possessed, mentally sorting through all the magical lessons I'd received in the hope I could remember something—anything—that might help. I felt so unbelievably helpless, and for the first time ever, regretted my stubbornness in fighting against learning more.

Aunt Millicent had been right.

She said I would regret not exploring my powers. She'd warned me that the day would come when I'd be facing a challenge and lose.

I was in that situation now, and there wasn't a damn thing I could do.

Except break the connection.

If I ended the spell and stopped the flow of power, the spirit couldn't stay inside her. He'd be cut off and too weakened to hold his position.

It was time to face the consequence.

If I survived, I would make sure I honored the legacy my family had passed down and not ignore it any more.

I took in a deep breath.

I looked to Micah.

"Go get Saundra Beaumont," I repeated again. Without another word, he left the room, and I whispered after him, "I love you. Forever."

Then I let go.

As I felt the electricity that had been part of the spell dissipate, I watched the residual energy from the mark be pulled out from my aunt, forming a grotesque mouth that opened wide in a ghoulish cry.

"They will come, and you will die. Praise be to the one I serve."

Then in an explosion of black, the marking disappeared.

Aunt Millicent crumpled to the side.

A price had been paid—a sacrifice made.

She was dead.

CHAPTER 14

$\mathcal{M}$y aunt's funeral was beautiful.

She would've been tickled pink by those who attended to pay her and our family respect. After the services, everyone had come to Shelf Indulgence for some light refreshments.

I walked around in a daze, numb with grief and denial.

She'd sacrificed herself for me. It had never been her intention to have me remove the threat. I could see that now. She'd opened herself up and taken on the mark herself. She'd wanted to spare me any further pain.

The mysterious attacker had killed her just for spite. I'd scoured the magical books I'd inherited to see what had happened, and the same answer kept coming back to me. The blood exchange shouldn't have resulted in her death. The spell was messy, but solid. It would've provided one hell of a kick, but never to this extent.

No, the more I looked at it from different perspectives, the more I knew the truth.

Aunt Millicent didn't deserve to die.

My head demanded justice.

My heart demanded vengeance.

I saw the side glances from those my aunt admired. They were members of the coven she had dedicated her life to. Even Roman Bishop had come to pay his respects.

"I'm sorry about your aunt, Sedona. She was a great woman." His words were all polished and sophisticated. I had a feeling this was the façade he presented to the world and was nothing like who he truly was. I'd heard whisperings. In a town like Havenwood Falls, people talked, and he was definitely a favorite topic to gossip about.

Roman Bishop was a man you never wanted to cross or get on the bad side of, and I was pretty sure he didn't care who Millicent Mathews was at all. This was all merely a formality—what you said at a funeral when you didn't have anything real to say.

"Thank you, sir," I answered respectfully.

He nodded brusquely and then walked away.

"People are starting to leave." Micah placed his hand at my elbow, letting me know that he was there. "Then I'll get you home."

Home was now Micah's house. I hadn't felt safe enough to return to the apartment, and I didn't have the heart to be upstairs. It was too soon. My feelings too raw. He and Holly had made sure to pack a few of my belongings and see that Lavender was brought over from my apartment.

Right now, all I wanted to do was curl up with my cat and sleep. Anything to avoid reality.

"I don't want to be here anymore," I whispered, after looking around at those who still remained. I didn't have the heart to listen to any more apologies over my loss of another family member, or how much the person would miss my aunt.

They were empty words that wouldn't bring her back.

"Breathe, sweetheart."

I leaned into him. "What would I do without you?" It was hard not to feel lost. I was an orphan now—my family gone. The weight of that almost suffocated me. "I can't stay. I need to go."

Tears were already falling as I fled Shelf Indulgence.

If only I had the courage to keep going.

IT WAS LATE when I arrived at the house. Lights were shining through one of the windows, showing at least someone was up.

My phone had blown up with texts and missed calls from Micah. I finally replied that I was okay, that I'd just needed to clear my head a bit.

The front door clicked closed behind me, and when I turned around to catch my breath, I was surprised to find not just Micah, but Holly and Maxwell sitting in the living room—all looking at me.

"Umm, hi?" I said with a small wave of my hand. It reminded me of an intervention I'd seen in a TV show. The way they studied my every move left me feeling nervous. Reading the atmosphere in the room, I could feel the love and concern they shared.

"Come in and talk with us," Maxwell replied, the aged ghost floating behind the couch Holly was sitting on. The poor girl looked tired, and a pang of guilt went through me for not coming home sooner.

"I kinda lost track of time," I continued, wanting to shake whatever this feeling was. Since seeing my aunt die before me, I'd been terrified to use any of my gifts. I hadn't been good enough—strong enough—to keep us all safe. "So I'm sorry."

"We understand, sweetheart." Micah stood up and came to where I was standing. Wrapping me up in his arms, he held me tight against him. The spell was truly gone, and I was back to feeling like regular old me. "But we do need to discuss what happened."

Tears filled my eyes again. Why would he want to rehash something that obviously hurt my heart?

"Please, it's too soon." I just couldn't find the words to form the sentences needed. It was all too much.

He rubbed the sides of my arms. I felt little comfort. "I know, but it's important. The magicked marking gave us a warning."

And there it was. The real reason behind this discussion. It wasn't so much about how I was reacting to the death, but more for the bomb he was about to level me with.

"Please don't say it," I cried. I was barely hanging on to my composure. If he uttered the words I knew were coming, it would completely break me.

His brows furrowed briefly. "I think we need to come up with a plan. Something is coming. Whether it's this Collector Austin was working for, or something else, we need to come up with a plan for when it arrives."

I hiccupped from the force of the sob that ripped from me. "You mean you're not leaving Havenwood Falls?"

I frantically looked over to Holly and Maxwell for confirmation. Sadness was the only thing I could sense radiating from them.

"Do you think we should?" The sincerity in his eyes spoke volumes. That wasn't what caught my attention, however.

"We?" I felt like I was stuck in a movie toward the end without a clue of what had happened beforehand. He'd said we—not just him and Holly.

"Do you really think I'd just leave you here?" Micah's eyes grew round. "Didn't you hear me say that I love you?"

I had heard it, but with everything in chaos, the sentiment had been shoved to the side. Wiping away my tears, I needed to tell him how I felt. "I love you, too. I also know how important it is to keep Holly safe, so I understand if you need to leave."

"We'd better not be leaving Havenwood Falls," came the indignant complaint from Micah's younger charge. Holly stood up and came toward me. "I finally feel like I can have a home here. I can go to school and live like a normal teenager." She folded her arms across her chest and defiantly glared at Micah. "So you can go, but I'm staying here with Sedona and Maxwell."

He didn't say a word for what seemed like a lifetime. "Do you feel the same way?" He'd directed his question to my ghostly friend.

I could tell Maxwell was chuffed about being included. "I haven't always approved of the men in Sedona's life, but you . . . you make her happy. Plus, I've developed a soft spot for a pretty young brunette with a voracious appetite for reading."

Holly blushed at the compliment. "I'd say you're outvoted, Uncle

Micah." We all knew they weren't related, but she hadn't given up the family endearment. "Three against one."

"Count again."

Even I had to look at him quizzically.

He grinned. "I mean it. It's not three against one. I want the same thing. I thought I'd have to convince Sedona here."

All eyes turned to me. I was so freaking happy right now, but there was still the bigger picture to consider. "But will you be safe if you stay?"

"Would we be safer if we left?" he countered, much to my annoyance.

"I'm being serious here. I love you so much, Micah, and can't imagine my life without you. But I won't claim happiness for myself at someone else's expense." I turned to Holly. "All I want is for you to have a chance to be normal. Magic is a weighty responsibility."

Holly came and hugged me. "And who better to help me learn my own powers than a badass empath who loves me?"

"This means you'll need to let go of your aversion to exploring your gifts," Maxwell chimed in, his eyebrow cocked as if to challenge me to disagree.

He was right. Things would definitely be different now. I'd already made the decision to follow my aunt's counsel and not hide away.

"So you'll stay in Havenwood Falls," I stated.

"And you'll live here with us," added Holly. Micah grinned in response.

"I'll continue helping out when I can," Maxwell contributed.

Holly wore a huge smile. "And I'll work at Shelf Indulgence after finishing school for the day. I can't wait to attend Havenwood Falls High."

That made Micah pause. "We still need to discuss that."

As they bantered back and forth, a new sensation settled over me. It wasn't replacing the grief I felt over what we lost or the apprehension I still had for the future. Threats still seemed to lurk around every corner, hiding in shadows.

It was contentment.

It was knowing that even when it felt like it, I wasn't truly alone. My friends had become family as well, and they surrounded me with their love and support. I still had the Beaumonts, and more than ever, I felt the need to reach out and be better at communicating with them.

Micah was at the center of that.

My angel.

I'd learned a lot over the past few months.

I'd faced many challenges.

But one thing was for sure—falling in love could be deadly for an empath.

But—as my mother realized before me—it was worth the risk.

We hope you enjoyed this story in the Havenwood Falls series featuring a variety of supernatural creatures. The series is a collaborative effort by multiple authors.

Other Havenwood Falls books by Belinda Boring:
Nowhere to Hide
The Collector: Awakening by Kristie Cook, R.K. Ryals, Belinda Boring & Nadirah Foxx
Blood and Damnation
Wrath and Retribution
Sun & Moon Academy Book One: Fall Semester
Sun & Moon Academy Book Two: Spring Semester

Also look for the YA line, Havenwood Falls High; the historical paranormal line, Legends of Havenwood Falls; the sexier side of town, Havenwood Falls Sin & Silk; the local supernatural college, Sun & Moon Academy; and the Havenwood Falls holiday short story anthologies.

Stay up to date at www.HavenwoodFalls.com

ABOUT THE AUTHOR

International and #1 Multi-Genre Bestselling Author Belinda Boring is known to many readers as the Queen of Swoon and also the Queen of Cliffhangers. Her Mystic Wolves series has topped many charts along with receiving several awards and nominations such as Paranormal Book of the Year, Best Debut Book, as well as being in the Top 3 Best Rated on Amazon. With additional titles like Bittersweet Melody, Bittersweet Symphony, Enchanted Hearts, Loving Liberty, and Broken Promises, it's easy to see why readers are captivated by this swoon-worthy author!

A homesick Aussie living amongst the cactus and mountains of Arizona, Belinda Boring is a self-proclaimed addict of romance and all things swoon-worthy. It wasn't long before she began writing, pouring her imagination and creativity into the stories she dreams. Whether urban fantasy, paranormal romance, or romance in general, Belinda strives to share great plots with heart and characters that you can't help but connect with. Of course, she wouldn't be Belinda without adding heroes she hopes will curl your toes. Surrounded by a supportive cast of family, friends, two adorable Chiweenies, and the man she gives her heart and soul to, Belinda is living the good life. Happy reading!

You can find Belinda on Social Media:
Official Website: www.belindaboringauthor.com/
Facebook: www.facebook.com/BelindaBoringAuthor
Twitter: twitter.com/BelindaBoring
Instagram: www.instagram.com/BelindaBoring
BookBub: www.bookbub.com/profile/belindaboring

ACKNOWLEDGMENTS

I wanted to say a quick, but VERY heartfelt thank you to everyone who has supported and stood by me throughout this year. I'm grateful for your love and friendships. I'm grateful for the inspiration you bring into my life and the way you embrace each and every one of my stories and characters.

I love writing within the Havenwood Falls world. Paranormal romance is one of my greatest loves—both to read and write—so I feel like I have the best of both worlds. There aren't enough words to express how much I appreciate author Kristie Cook and the exceptional authors I write alongside with. I remember reading countless quotes and articles about 'finding your tribe' and how much that can help as an author. Without a doubt, I've found my tribe, and I ADORE each and every single one of these talented writers. I cherish the friendships I've been able to make. You guys are the cream of the crop!

Thank you to those who work behind the scenes as I write:

My amazing author coach, Jessi Gibson. She helps me to keep focused when I have a STRONG tendency to squirrel. I love having her in my corner—cheering for me and keeping me accountable when I start doubting myself.

My faithful beta readers, Cindy Mayberry, Julie Engle, Julia Lucero, Susan McCray, and Stephanie Krause. Your feedback means a lot. Thank you!

The best writing partner a girl can have, Stephanie Garza. Our video writing sessions are some of the best memories I have, and I'm so grateful for you. We've written a lot of words this year. I can't wait to see what 2019 holds.

My family: Thank you for always asking how my writing is going and being excited when I finish a story. It might not seem like much, but to me, it is. I love you all!

My incredible husband, Mark. You're the reason behind it all. Whatever I did to deserve you . . . I'd do it a thousand times again and again. You always seem to know what I need, when I need it. You help me remember my words. You listen to me when I'm stuck and have to talk the scene through. Most of all, you never complain when we listen to Hamilton and *In The Heights* on repeat. You get me. You support me. You give me the space I need to be creative. Me and you forever . . . *that would be enough*! << shameless plug of a Hamilton lyric.

Lastly, because we save the best for last, right? All my love and gratitude to you all—those who pick up my books and agree to take the journey with me and my characters. Thank you for entrusting me with your time and imagination. Thank you for embracing my characters. You guys are AMAZING!

As always, don't be afraid to take a risk and dare to fly!

Happy swooning!

Bels xxx

AN EXCERPT

A Havenwood Falls New Adult Novella

HAVENWOOD FALLS

AFFLICTION MINE

USA Today Bestselling Author

C.J. PINARD

Affliction Mine (A Havenwood Falls Novel) by C.J. Pinard

At his cousin's pleading, Karson Kane returns to Havenwood Falls to help with his elven uncle, who's about to be released from supernatural prison. Karson has no idea what awaits him in the mysterious mountain town, but he feels strongly he's meant to go.

Within the first twenty-four hours, Karson's cousin gets thrown in jail, too, and Karson ends up in the ER, leaving him to think he may have made a mistake coming to the magical town. Until he meets Scottlin Glover. The gorgeous, auburn-haired breath of fresh air treats his injuries, but leaves him wanting more from her, as he can't seem to take his eyes off her.

Scottlin is very intrigued by the elven. Being only half human, she has ways to both heal and help, but she can't figure out how to help Karson when they realize there's something terribly wrong with him beyond the initial injury.

Karson begins to suspect that he has been lured to Havenwood Falls under false pretenses, but can't seem to find any answers. If he and Scottlin can't put their scorching attraction aside and heal Karson, the consequences will be more serious than they imagined—and very permanent.

AFFLICTION MINE

BY C.J. PINARD

The backpack was getting heavy, and I shifted it to my other shoulder as I wondered just where the hell this Greyhound bus was. It was supposed to depart at 10:20 a.m., but as of yet, it wasn't even here in the station.

"Karson! Hey, dude!"

I turned around and spotted my coworker, Dex, waving at me.

Oh, God, what does this guy want? I wondered as I watched him approach.

"Happy new year. Where you going, man?" he asked, staring at me as he took a swig from a black and green can.

"Going out of town. Why are you here?" I asked, keeping it vague so he'd go away.

"Same. Goin' to see family. You know." He shook his head before taking another swig of his caffeine-loaded drink as he measured me with a curious stare.

Seriously hoping this pothead wasn't on the same bus as me, I smiled tightly at him and said, "Great. Well, see you next week." I turned and headed toward the vending machines that lined the back of the Greyhound station.

Just as I was about to choose a bag of jalapeño-flavored potato chips, the loudspeaker announced that the bus to Montrose was leaving. I quickly shoved my dollar bill into the machine and willed the bag to drop so I could board the damn bus.

Once I snatched the chips from the bottom of the machine, I hustled to the boarding area, presented my ticket, and found a seat in the back, just wanting this stupid trip to be over with. I had other shit to attend to, and dealing with my "cousin" and his weird-ass request wasn't what I had on the agenda for the holidays.

Still . . . I literally couldn't remember when I had last been to Havenwood Falls. A part of me wondered why most of my childhood was absent from my memory, but I knew it had to do with the sleepy Colorado town. Had I really grown up there?

I pulled out my phone and clicked on the email app, deciding to re-read the cryptic message for the hundredth time.

Karson,

This is going to sound weird as hell, but hear me out. I need you to return to Havenwood Falls like, yesterday. I know you're thinking, "Return? When was I there?" Well, you have been here. You grew up here. You don't remember because the town is full of witches and other supes and shit. You leave, you don't get the luxury of remembering it at all. The witch bitches are gonna have my ass for telling you this, but I don't have any fucks left to give at this point, so here goes.

My pops, your uncle, is in a bad way. He used his affliction to piss off the Court and was sent to prison. Why am I telling you this? Because he's gotta do six weeks in jail here before they release him back to us. Before you ask why you should care, here's why: My dad's a loose cannon. In his late 40s and still ain't learned shit about shit. I need you to help me put a leash on him once he gets out. The Kane name has been muddied enough. Oh, and also, your dad is here (they're brothers), and he's been asking about you. It's getting old, and you need to come home. Of course, you prob don't remember your dad, but still.

Fuck . . . I know this email is so damn weird to you, but you have to trust me, cuz. Head up to Havenwood Falls, and you'll see.

Once you get here, your memories will return. All of them. It'll take a hot minute, but I promise it'll happen. It's gonna be a trip, bro. Take a bus to Montrose, and when you get off, there will be a special bus to Havenwood Falls at the stop there. Hop on it, and don't ask any questions. I'll swing by and get you at the coffee shop, which is the last stop for the bus. We'll talk then. Reply with your itinerary, dude. I need you here pronto.

Jalen

My head was spinning. The email had literally come out of nowhere yesterday, and the only reason I sat on this damn bus right now was pure, unadulterated curiosity. I hit reply on the email and told him I was on the bus heading to Montrose, but had no idea when I'd actually reach Havenwood Falls, as there was no online schedule to the place that I could find.

But the part of the email that touched on getting my memory back and the mention of my father had definitely sweetened the deal. As a twenty-four-year-old living on my own, I'd always taken care of number one. Nobody had ever been there to help me. I knew I had parents, but I could never get ahold of them. They never answered my texts or calls. I looked down at my phone and clicked the *Contacts* icon. Sure, I could click on *Dad*, but I knew it would go to a generic voicemail box.

It always did.

Hell, I couldn't even remember what my parents looked like or their names.

Then the email from this Jalen guy came in, promising me answers. It would have been a cold day in hell before I'd turn that down. I had no idea if he was shitting me or not, but hell, I'd take the chance. I had to. What did I have to lose, really? I was tired of wandering aimlessly, no matter how busy I was, always wondering if I had a family.

Half of me was hopeful this Jalen character was telling the truth and could fill in the missing pieces I felt had been absent from my brain. The other half of me was terrified that someone was playing a joke on me—that someone was running a hustle, and I would, yet again, be caught up in some shit I should have just walked away from. I had been lucky the guy hadn't pressed charges that night in the bar when I let my temper get the better of me over a stupid game of pool.

I pushed that from my mind and continued to click. I had to clear out my emails, because once I reached this mystery town, I knew I'd have no time for shit.

The next email to pop up on my phone was from a particularly needy client. Willing my eye to not twitch before I opened it, I took a deep breath and began to read:

Karson!

I want a Smurf. I need a Smurf! On my ass, or maybe my inner thigh ;) I know you can pull it off, can't you, cutie? ~Angel

I swallowed down my irritation and decided not to even reply. I deleted Angel's email and hoped she'd get the hint that I didn't want to tattoo her.

Ever.

A few weeks ago, she'd come into my shop in downtown Colorado Springs, tagging along with a friend. The friend was pleasant enough, just wanting a small tattoo of something to commemorate her father's passing. It was an easy tat, but what wasn't easy was the friend, Angel, who'd sat and stared at me as I worked. Sure, she'd pretended to be looking through the photo albums of my designs, but I knew she was checking me out. I could feel the weight of her stare as I tatted her friend.

When the friend's tattoo was done, she had been very happy with it, and paid me and thanked me profusely. Angel, though, asked me for my number. In deflection, I'd referred her to the front counter, where Dex would have given her a business card with the email address to our general box.

The crazy bitch used it, too. She'd sent me no less than six emails with photos of tattoos she wanted, and then suggested we meet up "in private" to talk about them.

Shouldn't I have been flattered? I guessed I should have. But at this time in my life, I didn't want to deal with such entanglements. Angel was hot, but I wasn't into pushy women. I was the one who called the shots.

I eventually drifted to sleep, and was awoken hours later when the bus driver indicated over the loudspeaker the stop we'd just reached: Montrose.

The cold air hit me like a slap in the face as I hopped off the bus and looked around. A truck stop of some kind greeted me. There were gas pumps and a large, convenience-type store with a red and yellow logo.

Not seeing any buses marked Havenwood Falls, I adjusted my backpack and wandered into the store. I needed to take a piss, anyway. The restrooms were clearly marked, and after I used the facilities, I went to wander around the shop, wondering what I should do next. I was starving, so I bought a premade sandwich and a bottle of Mountain Dew, along with a bag of beef jerky. I spied a small sitting area, and made my way toward it to eat my dinner. The bus ride had taken twice as long as it would have if I'd driven, and I'd only had the chips.

On my way to the tables, I passed a rack of brochures boasting all Colorado had to offer for recreation and tourism. A brochure for Telluride caught my eye. Something about the way the mountains in the photo were positioned in a box canyon intrigued me. Flicking my gaze away from it to make sure I wouldn't run into anything as I walked, my plan was to set my food down and come back for it. But as my gaze shifted back to the brochure, I thought my eyes were playing tricks on me; for where I could swear it had read "Telluride," it now read "Havenwood Falls."

What in the hell?

Of course, I immediately snatched the pamphlet from its resting place and quickly made my way to the tables, never taking my eyes off it. I blindly unwrapped my sandwich and bit into it as I set the pamphlet down on the table and unfolded it. Its glossy photos called out to me. As I stared at it, a knowing feeling began to swirl in my gut.

I'd seen that canyon before. Everything inside of me said I had been there before. I knew it deep down in my soul.

I opened the first page of the brochure, and my stomach began to turn over even more. Photos of familiar scenes seemed to jump off the page and smack me in the face. I knew that ski resort. I knew that inn. I knew those waterfalls. I knew that town square. And I most definitely knew that fucking tattoo shop.

My eyes scanned every inch of it, and when I flipped to the back, bright yellow writing caught my eye: *Buses to Havenwood Falls depart daily at 12 noon and 12 midnight.*

A glance at my watch showed 8:57 p.m.

Looked like I had three hours to kill, because come hell or high water, I would be on that bus.

After surfing the web, checking social media, and people-watching, a couple hours had passed, and I was getting anxious. I grabbed my bag, got up, and wandered over to the corner of the store.

I approached a store employee who was stocking coffee mugs bearing various Colorado logos and pictures. "Excuse me, can you tell me where the Havenwood Falls bus stops?"

She turned around, a mug in her hand. She dipped her eyebrows in confusion. "I'm sorry, I don't understand what you're asking me."

She seemed nice enough, but her response frustrated me. "Havenwood Falls—you have a bus departing at midnight. Does it meet out front? Is it marked?"

She shook her head. "I . . . I don't know where that is, so I can't help you. But maybe my manager knows. I can go get him—"

I pulled out the pamphlet and practically shoved it in her face. "See?"

She narrowed her eyes at it, then looked at me. With a shake of her head, she said, "That says Telluride. That bus meets out back. It's clearly marked."

I pulled the brochure back to my face to see it did, indeed, say Telluride on it.

What in the . . . ?

Feeling like I was going crazy, I checked my watch to see it was 11:51 p.m. I left the store and went around to the back, where a large bus depicting a mountain scene with *Havenwood Falls* written on it sat idling, no passengers on board, just one driver seated up front. I looked around to see if anyone else was in the parking lot, but it was deathly quiet.

I suddenly realized I didn't have a ticket, but I approached the bus anyway. The door was open, so I stepped inside and looked at the driver. He smiled at me with warm, brown eyes and waved me on, his face crinkling at the corners of his eyes. "Welcome!"

"Um, hi. Thanks. Where is this bus headed to?" I asked cautiously, remembering how the lady inside the truck stop couldn't see the brochure the same way I had.

"Well, where do you want to go?" he asked jovially, his pale skin looking almost sickly under the one orange light illuminating the parking lot.

Here goes nothing. "Havenwood Falls?"

"Well, you've come to the right place, elf. Choose a seat, and we'll be on our way!"

I blinked at him a few times before quickly checking my reflection in the large overhead mirror at the front of the bus. I was glad to see my glamour hadn't slipped, as the driver had given me a strange look. Sighing, I pushed a stray blond strand from my forehead and looked at him.

The old driver grinned at me and then looked down at the newspaper he'd been reading. At that moment, the only thought I had was to exit the bus and just run. Hitchhike, Uber . . . something, and get the hell out of Montrose and go back to my mundane life. But something even stronger than fear was pulling at me to stay on that bus.

So without another glance at the driver, I took a seat in the middle of the bus, set my backpack on the seat next to me, and blew out a breath. To my surprise, the driver closed the door, put the bus in gear, and began to drive. I glanced at my phone to see it was midnight on the dot.

Feeling weird that I was the only passenger, but too tired to give a shit, I used my backpack as a makeshift pillow and quickly fell asleep.

The first thing I felt was cold. As I blinked my eyes open, I could see I was still seated on the bus, I was alone, and it was dark outside. The door was folded open, but the driver was gone. I wiped drool from the corner of my mouth and stretched.

After wearily grabbing my bag, I made my way down the aisle, and off the bus. As I stepped down, I could see I was in front of the coffee shop Jalen had told me about. The January air was chilly as hell, and I was only in a hoodie and jeans.

With my breath pluming out in front of me in foggy puffs, I hurried toward the shop and hoped it was still open. But judging by the darkness behind the windows, I wasn't optimistic. So I wasn't surprised when I tried to pull open the front door to Broastful Brew and it was locked up tight.

The hissing sound of air brakes caused me to turn my head. I saw the bus's doors close and its wheels turn, pulling away from the coffee shop.

"Shit," I murmured, wondering what I was going to do now.

Purchase *Affliction Mine* where books are sold.